The Times

'Taut and suspense packed right up to the last page.'
The Financial Times

'A fast-paced thriller in which nothing is as it seems.'
The Independent

'A beautifully crafted complex thriller.'
The Independent on Sunday

'A gripping story, impossible to put down.
Green cranks up the tension with every page.'
L. A. Weatherly, bestselling author of *Angel*

Recommended by Radio 4 Open Book

Praise for Caroline Green's *Dark Ride*:

Winner of the RoNA Young Adult Award

'...ll of tension, mystery and real-life drama,
Dark Ride is not to be missed.' *Chicklish*

'Almost impossible to put down.' *Goodreads*

Caroline Green is an experienced freelance journalist who has written stories since she was a little girl. She vividly remembers a family walk when she was ten years old where she was so preoccupied with thoughts of her new 'series' that she almost walked into a tree.

Caroline lives in North London with her husband, two sporty sons and one very bouncy Labrador retriever.

Her first novel, *Dark Ride*, was longlisted for the Branford Boase Award and won the RoNA Young Adult Award. Her second novel, *Cracks*, has received high critical acclaim and fan praise.

hold your breath

Caroline Green

PICCADILLY PRESS

To Mia, Andrew, Jennie,
Alex, Christine, Trudy,
Rowan, Luke, Ben and Lily
from East Barnet School.

First published in Great Britain in 2013
by Piccadilly Press Ltd
A Templar/Bonnier publishing company
Deepdene Lodge, Deepdene Avenue,
Dorking, Surrey, RH5 4AT, UK
www.piccadillypress.co.uk

A catalogue record for this book is available
from the British Library

ISBN: 978 1 84812 170 6 (paperback)

Also available as an ebook

1 3 5 7 9 10 8 6 4 2

Printed in the UK by CPI Group (UK), Croydon, CR0 4YY
Cover design by Simon Davis
Cover photo © gifyo.com/wickedlace

PROLOGUE

The blackness began to dissolve. She tried to move her head but pain jack-hammered inside her skull and nausea gripped her stomach. Closing her eyes, she willed the sensations to pass.

Minutes went by. Or was it longer? Time didn't seem to run in a straight line any more but looped and rolled back on itself. When she opened her eyes again her bottom lip was smushed against something damp and cold. Raising her head and blinking heavy, sticky eyes, she saw that she was lying on a duvet with a faded pattern of daisies and that she had been drooling on it. Coldness had seeped through the duvet from the hard floor beneath it. Groaning, she forced her body up onto her elbows. Her head hurt everywhere, but one part of her scalp throbbed with bright urgency. She drew her tongue over dry lips, tasting blood; it felt swollen and oversized in her mouth.

She rolled onto her back and discovered her wrists and her ankles were bound with strong plastic ties. A single lightbulb hung in the middle of a ceiling above her, its glow sickly in the gloom. Familiar . . . but why?

A wooden chair, heaped with blankets, was opposite her. Then the blankets moved.

'Are you awake?'

The hissing voice kicked her heartbeat faster. She could see now that there was a figure there, sitting upright, hands folded between their knees.

'Well, are you?'

She hoped she was asleep. Then she would wake up in her own bedroom with sunlight soaking through her curtains.

But hot tears slid down her face because she knew this nightmare was really happening.

CHAPTER 1

KEYS

'We're going to be late!'

'I know, I know! Oh for God's sake, has anyone seen my keys?' Mum bustled into the room in a cloud of perfume, her kitten heels tapping the stone tiles with a staccato rhythm.

Tara met her mother's eyes for just a second. But it was long enough. She turned her attention back to the screen of the laptop.

'Tara?'

'Nope,' she said flatly. 'No idea where they are.'

Mum sighed and left the room.

Tara knew the cocktail of emotions her mother was

feeling. Relieved, because Tara hadn't done her 'thing', yet wishing she'd been able to locate the missing keys all the same.

As they say, it was complicated.

She looked down at the maths problem in her homework and breathed slowly. Distraction, that's what she needed in these moments. Focus on something else. She was getting good at it. Then Beck turned his music right up and both her parents yelled, 'Turn it down!' at the same time. Tara's concentration shattered.

The inside of a pocket. A rain jacket. A crumpled tissue. The packet of cigarettes that Mum thought no one knew about. Nestled beneath them, the keys with the sparkly heart charm lying at the top.

Dad spoke, bringing her attention sharply back to the room.

'What were you wearing yesterday?' he said, his voice taut with irritation.

'Well,' said Mum, 'I popped out to get milk at teatime. It was raining a bit . . .'

'So maybe your cagoule?' Dad was the only person in the world who referred to a rain jacket as a cagoule. Tara felt a squeeze of affection, despite the queasy feeling in her stomach. At this rate, they'd be late for their anniversary meal and it would be her fault. She contemplated opening her mouth and freeing the words stacked up there. 'Mum, your keys are in your *cagoule.*' But she knew it would prompt quick, alarmed glances between her and Dad. *This again? Didn't we think Tara had stopped this?*

But thankfully she didn't have to say anything.

'Oh!' said her mother. 'Now there's a thought . . .'

A few minutes later the keys had been located. Mum and Dad yelled goodbye and the door closed behind them. Tara could imagine the conversation only too well.

'I really think she's grown out of that phase now, thank God. Don't you?'

'I told you it would only take time. The whole sorry episode is best forgotten.'

Yes, Dad, she thought. *Let's just pretend none of it happened. Let's pretend Tara's normal. And that no one ever got hurt.*

Beck came into the room then. One hand was rummaging inside his jeans, as usual. The other held a can of Coke, which he scrunched up and tossed into the bin before burping roundly.

'You're disgusting,' Tara said, wrinkling her nose.

He grinned, flashing his perfect teeth. His green eyes twinkled. Tara snorted and turned back to the computer screen. That cheeky smile might charm most of the female population between the ages of ten and eighty but it didn't work on her.

'Right, I'm offski,' he said, snatching up his jacket from the back of the chair.

'But you said you were staying in tonight!' She couldn't control the desperation that clung to her words.

Beck shrugged. 'Had a better offer. Anyway, you don't need babysitting, do you?'

'No, but you told Mum and Dad you'd —'

'Oh come on, Tar,' he said in a bored voice. 'You might want to sit in every night like some sort of nun, but some of us have a life.'

'Get lost then,' she said tightly.

'Look, I didn't mean to —'

'Off you go,' she interrupted. 'I don't care what you do anyway.'

She turned back to the computer screen.

A few minutes later she heard the front door close again.

Tara gazed at the screen but the homework may as well have been in hieroglyphics. The numbers began to swim and distort and she knew that one of those horrible headaches was coming. They always did after she'd 'found' something. Even though she hadn't even been *trying* to find Mum's keys. Which was pretty unfair.

Getting out of the chair, Tara stretched, trying to free the tightness in her neck and shoulders. Mum was always telling her off for her posture. She raised her fingertips into the air as high as she could, her T-shirt riding up and exposing her waist. A memory of Jay's warm hand on the small of her back at the pool party loomed out of nowhere. She caught her breath at how much this still hurt, despite everything else that had happened.

Some of us have a life, Beck had said.

Maybe other people deserved one.

Beck had no idea what it was like to be her. To have guilt gnawing at your insides every single day. A wave of bitterness washed over Tara then and she swore. The word rang out, loud and satisfying, in the empty house.

A walk, she decided. She'd get out of here for a while and try to walk off the headache and the bad thoughts.

'Sammie!' she called. 'Here, boy.'

Their yellow Labrador trotted into the room, brown eyes hopeful and tail wagging with a metronome beat. Tara smiled and went to the cupboard to get his lead. When Jay had been pushing her further with whispered promises and urgent kisses last summer, she'd lain on the back lawn, arm slung across Sammie's furry back. The dog had slumbered peacefully next to her and Tara had felt like the smelly old mutt was the only loved-one in her life who didn't put any pressure on her.

Their shadows stretched long and thin in the low evening sun as Tara and Sammie headed down the alley near the house. It led to the river, which ran all the way into the centre of town.

It was the beginning of October and everyone was talking about an Indian summer. The weather veered from unseasonal heat to thundery rain from day to day. But tonight, the air felt soft and warm on the bare skin of her arms and the edgy feeling inside Tara began to calm a little.

A duck skimmed onto the water with a creaky quack, sending a long V-shape in its wake. The long grasses at the side of the river were tangled with the remnants of wildflowers, humming with insect life, and the trees opposite were mirrored on the still surface of the water.

Tara took slow, deep breaths of the sweet air.

A mother and a small girl on a bike were coming towards her and she stood to one side, allowing them past. She got out her phone and pretended to text someone. She always looked away when small children were around. But it was hard to ignore this one, with her over-the-top bike. It was festooned with ribbons and a bunch of bells, which looked like the sort that came with chocolate Easter rabbits. The bells *ting-ting*ed as the girl trundled by, fat knees pumping away.

'I zooming, Mummy,' said the little girl proudly.

'Yes, lovey, you are,' said the woman, swooping her weary eyes up and grinning at Tara. Tara smiled back weakly and then let her gaze slide quickly away as they passed.

'C'mon, Samster,' she said, too loud, slapping her thigh. The dog was engaged in some vigorous sniffing action in the bushes but happily trotted over at the sound of her voice.

Walking along with her dog in the warm air helped the knots of tension in her muscles and mind begin to loosen. She reached into her pocket for her iPod. Soon she was humming along to Kings of Leon, her feet moving in easy rhythm to the pounding beat.

She liked walking along the river. It always calmed her.

In fact, she didn't mind living in this new town. Not that she had made any friends but, for now, being anonymous was the very best she could hope for. She dreaded someone knowing *someone* who knew *someone* at her old school.

If anyone asked, the official reason for the move was that Dad had got a new, better-paid job and it meant relocating fifty miles north of where Tara had grown up. But there was another, unspoken reason. No one knew them here. There would be no sly stares when she went into town. No whispers behind her back at school.

No one here knew about a little boy called Tyler Evans.

The music was loud and she was engrossed in thought, so when someone walked past close enough to brush her arm, she yelped, yanking out her earbuds.

'God!' she said. 'You scared me!' Her shocked heartbeat echoed into her throat and her cheeks flushed.

A tall boy, a little older than her, was regarding her with a surprised expression.

'Sorry,' he said gruffly. 'I said *s'cuse*, but you didn't hear me.' He had close-cropped dark hair and navy blue eyes with enviable lashes. He was wearing a white T-shirt that showed tanned arms with curving muscles and low-slung jeans. Almost gorgeous, but with an arrogant moodiness that was a turn-off. He looked like he loved himself a little too much. He took a step back as Sammie bounded over to say hello. 'Whoa . . .' His hands were up now, his lips drawn into a tight line.

'He's just being friendly,' said Tara. *What a wimp,* she thought. *Fancy being scared of Sammie.*

The boy muttered something and hurried off, checking

his mobile as he went. There was a single word written on the back of his T-shirt. *Lifeguard.*

The dog looked as though he had every intention of chasing after the boy in an attempt to bond with him further.

'Sammie!' barked Tara harshly. 'Play dead!' It was one of the many commands Dad had painstakingly trained the dog to do as a puppy. But it was the only one he'd trained him to do successfully. Calls of 'Sit!' and 'Fetch!' were met with looks of stubborn resistance.

Sammie flumped down onto his belly and placed his head on his paws.

'Good boy,' said Tara. She clipped on the lead and sat down on a bench, watching the boy disappear around the bend in the river. He had that air about him, of someone who thought he was a bit of a Hard Man. She knew his type. She didn't like really short hair on boys either. Much nicer to have something to twist your fingers into. Like Jay's hair. It was impossible not to think about the way it curled into his neck now. And his sparkly brown eyes, which always seemed to contain some vaguely naughty knowledge.

Tara sighed deeply. When would thoughts like that stop bugging her?

The list of *Things Tara Didn't Want To Think About* was getting longer by the day. She wished she'd listened to her friends at the time. Hadn't they warned her about Jay Burns? She was just another notch. That's all. Nothing special about her, despite all the things he'd said about her being 'like no one else'. That was probably true, she thought. But not in a good way.

Irritated to find tears pricking her eyes, she found a tissue in her pocket and blew her nose, then tried to rub away the leaky mascara that had somehow strayed under her eyelids.

Coming here was a fresh start. In future she was going to keep her heart locked away. She wouldn't let herself get hurt like that again.

Getting up, Tara looked up the river path and wondered whether she should just go home. But she was thirsty and remembered there was a row of shops up the road a bit, off the river. She'd buy a can of something to drink first. An evening alone in front of the telly wasn't something she was in a rush to do.

She carried on walking and turned the corner, where a distinctive iron bridge covered the river. Standing in the dark curve underneath, where the bricks were stained green and the river usually smelt like drains, was the boy who had passed her before. Tara's steps slowed down. He wasn't alone. Voices echoed off the walls. The words were indistinct, but clearly full of anger and heat.

A girl was leaning in towards him, her face pushed so close to his they must have been breathing each others' air.

Oh, thought Tara with a sinking feeling, recognising her.

Melodie Stone. The biggest bitch in her class.

Melodie had sleek golden hair and a mean, pretty face.

She always had the top of her school skirt turned over that extra inch, one more button on her shirt undone than anyone else. Tara had accidentally sat in her seat on her first week at school. Melodie had looked at her as though she was pond life, lip curled and eyes bright with malice. She hadn't even spoken, but had waited until someone else pointed out Tara's 'mistake'. Tara had been tempted to stay put but decided there was no point making enemies on her first day. In the few weeks since then, Tara had heard some of her withering put-downs to other people. Once, Melodie had almost reduced their mousey art teacher, Mrs Henderson, to tears. It was probably best that she'd taken a deep breath and moved seats that day. She didn't need the hassle.

Tara sat behind Melodie in English and was therefore in prime position to witness the tedious way Melodie lifted up her silky mane of hair before letting it swing back again, like she was in some shampoo advert. She'd caught Tara watching her once and given her an annoying, slow smile as though saying, 'Gorgeous, aren't I? Unlike you.' Tara had swooped her eyes and looked away again, cheeks flaming.

Melodie was at the centre of a group Tara privately called the Gossip Girls, because they seemed to think they'd just walked off the set of some shiny American TV programme. Some of them even had ratty little handbag dogs. She tried to keep out of their way. An air of meanness hung about them, as strong as their perfume. She didn't want to give them an excuse to pick on her.

Tara's step slowed now as the argument increased in volume. Melodie's hand snapped up so fast it was almost a blur. The boy put his hand to his cheek, said something quietly with a vicious expression and stalked away in the other direction, hands in his pockets and head slung low.

Melodie Stone fumbled in her handbag and produced a pack of cigarettes. With a shaking hand she lit one up and inhaled deeply. She spotted Tara then and fixed her with a dead-eyed look.

'Er, are you okay?' said Tara uncertainly.

Melodie barked a sudden harsh laugh that made Tara flinch.

'Yeah, I'm completely *brilliant*,' she said, blowing smoke sideways out of her mouth. 'And it's none of your business anyway. Why don't you get lost?'

'Pardon me for breathing!' said Tara, turning back the other way. 'I'm sorry I asked.'

Rattled and hot, she headed home.

Sammie looked up at his mistress anxiously as she marched along, picking up on her irritation. Tara wished she'd turned back before Melodie had seen her. She'd probably have it in for her on Monday morning because Tara had witnessed her stupid row with her idiot boyfriend. It was all she needed right now.

But that was one problem Tara didn't have to deal with.

Because when she went to school again on Monday, Melodie Stone was gone.

CHAPTER 2

NORMAL

The first she knew about it was when she spotted Jada Morgan from her class huddled with her cronies in a way that transmitted 'drama'. Jada was snivelling loudly but Tara noted she didn't have a red nose or piggy eyes like normal people got from crying. She held perfectly French-manicured fingers under her brimming eyelids, catching the jewels of her tears before they damaged her foundation.

'But why didn't she just *tell* us?' wailed Jada. This seemed to be the tipping point for another girl, Amber, who started to sob.

'All I got was this!' Jada held up her pink BlackBerry.

She wiggled it from side to side like it would talk.

'Lemme see again,' said Karis Jones, taking the phone and studying the message.

Tara took her time finding her PE kit in her locker. It was hard not be curious.

'*Babes,*' read Karis in a slow, serious tone. '*Gotta go away. Love U all. Kisses to my girls.*'

Jada's sobbing went up a notch.

'I'm going to miss her, so, so much,' said Chloe Simmons, a girl with big moist eyes and long hair she constantly chewed.

Tara yanked out the PE kit and walked past the huddle in the corridor. She accidentally caught the eye of Karis, who glared at her, but Tara had to fight back a smirk.

Today was definitely looking up.

Variations of the same conversation buzzed around her all day like static.

'Have you heard? Melodie Stone has left.'

'What, just like that?'

'Yeah, just like that.'

Their form tutor made an announcement at registration saying that Melodie had had a family issue to deal with and would be living with relatives in Brighton for the foreseeable future.

This prompted more hysteria from Jada.

Mrs Linley rolled her eyes in irritation. 'Try and contain your grief a little, please, Jada,' she said, prompting disgusted tuts from the rest of the Gossip

Girls who snaked thin, bangled arms around their quivering friend.

The whole thing was a bit strange, Tara thought. People didn't usually just up and disappear in the middle of term. Although . . . that was exactly what Tara had done at her old school. But that was a unique circumstance.

She wondered if the scene she'd witnessed with lover boy under the bridge had been him trying to persuade her not to go. But who cared, really? She couldn't say she was going to be missing Melodie Stone.

As far as Tara was concerned, it was good riddance.

The end of the day came around and Tara hung back in her English class, hoping to avoid the crush in the corridors as everyone shoved and jockeyed to get to their lockers. She always hated that part of the day, when plans bounced like shuttlecocks around her head. 'See you later at blah-blah,' and 'Everyone's going, it'll be great!'

Tara was never going and none of them ever saw her later.

She felt someone's gaze and looked up to see her English teacher, Mr Ford, watching her.

'Everything all right, Tara?' he said.

'Um, fine thanks.' She quickly gathered up the rest of her stuff and hurried out into the corridor. It was still heaving so she went to the girls' loos and locked herself in the least undesirable cubicle for a while to kill some more time. She played with her mobile and, despite herself, wished she hadn't deleted all Jay's messages.

After a while she emerged into the corridor, which was surprisingly empty. She hunkered down to decant some books into her locker, wishing as always that it wasn't so awkwardly placed. Arriving late in the school year meant she had to put up with one of the rubbish lower lockers. Melodie's had been head height – perfectly placed. Of course. She was that sort of girl, the one who always managed to get the advantage. Her locker was just above Tara's. Many times, Tara'd had to wait for Miss-Loves-Herself to finish up before she could get near her own. She swore Melodie sometimes took ages on purpose.

She glanced up at the locker now.

A nervous feeling suddenly fluttered in her stomach for no reason at all, followed by a rapid drumbeat in her chest. That was weird. What was making her feel like this?

Everything around Melodie's locker seemed oddly in shadow, as though at the periphery of Tara's vision. She was suddenly seized by an overwhelming urge to look in Melodie's locker, which was ridiculous. No, she didn't *want* to at all. But she felt that she *needed* to somehow. It made absolutely no sense. But she had to do it all the same.

Tara licked her lips. Her mouth had gone desert dry. She looked around the corridor. A cleaner was sloshing a mop about at the far end, headphones on, eyes cast down. No one was looking at her. No one would know.

She looked at the locker again. It wasn't open, of course, but these lockers were the same kind as at her old school and, if there was no padlock, easy to open. A boy called Alexi had showed her how to open them with a hairgrip in Year Seven when hers had got jammed. On autopilot, she fumbled in her pocket. Her long black hair was in a ponytail today and she had no hairgrips. She remembered the compass in her pencil case. Hurriedly getting it out, she pushed the sharp tip into the keyhole and jiggled it a little, feeling something give.

She looked around again. A couple of Sixth Formers who were laughing at something on a mobile phone walked towards her. She waited until they passed, pretending to adjust her earring. Then, when she was sure no one was watching, she gently pushed the door open with a cautious finger. She didn't know why she was doing this. It was definitely weird behaviour. And 'weird' was a place that she, Tara Murray, was trying to leave behind. But still she looked.

There was nothing much to see though. The inside of the door held a poster of an actor from a gruesome vampire show on telly, all shirtless and glistening with oil. A body spray lay on its side and its musky aroma clung to the space. It reminded Tara instantly of Melodie and, for a second, the sensation that she was close by was so strong that Tara swung round to look behind her. But no one was there. She turned back to the locker. A single pink sweet had melted against the metal wall. Some sort of paper was wedged at the back, all bunched up. Tara tentatively poked her hand inside and reached for it, giving it a pull to free it from where it was trapped by the metal casing.

A strip of photo booth pictures showed Melodie, her hair piled on top of her head, messy but attractively arranged. She was with an older boy with a small dark beard and a wolfish expression. The first three pictures showed Melodie laughing and sticking her head close to the camera or making faces, the boy in the background smiling indulgently. The final picture showed him with his face buried in Melodie's neck, kissing her while she looked at the camera with a cat-got-the-cream expression.

Suddenly feeling stalkerish and pervy, Tara dropped the photo. There was something else in the locker . . . a tiny silver earring shaped like a treble clef. She picked it up and ran her thumb over the smooth metal. The spicy body spray aroma became stronger now and then something else took over: the artificial strawberry smell of the melted sweet clung to the insides of her nostrils, cloying, choking. The interior of the locker went dark and then Tara was all nerve endings. Smells, colour, tastes all battered her and intricate patterns swam before her eyes. Staggering backwards, she barely felt the sharp corner of the locker door scraping the soft flesh of her inner arm. She stumbled until she felt the wall and she sat heavily on a bench, hands over her eyes. The jumbled pictures and white noise started to clear into an image in her mind.

And then it was blindingly detailed, like a screen where Tara could see every individual pixel.

A gloomy room. A single lightbulb swaying above her. A rotten, dank smell. Hard to . . . breathe . . . I'm scared . . .

'Tara?'

A blinding white light seared across her vision and then cleared to reveal the craggy, concerned face of Mr Ford, peering down at her.

'What's wrong? Are you ill?'

'No!' Tara's voice came out thin and small as she struggled to her feet. 'I'm all right . . . Oh.' Something warm hit the skin of her upper foot. She looked down. Blood plopped from her arm and trickled down her foot in a crimson rivulet.

'You're evidently not all right, young lady! You're bleeding!' Mr Ford took her gently by the other arm and passed her a large cotton handkerchief, which she pressed against the cut. 'Now come with me to the medical room.'

'But —'

'No buts!'

Tara let herself be led down the corridor, through the fire doors at the end, and up two floors to the medical room. The nurse/secretary had gone for the day, so Mr Ford busied himself with antiseptic wipes and plasters on a roll while Tara meekly waited, wishing she didn't feel so sick and that the throbbing in her head would stop.

He expertly cleaned and bandaged her arm. She managed to avoid meeting his eye throughout the whole process, although he was close enough for her to smell coffee on his breath.

'There,' he said after a little while. 'That should do it.'

She looked up and met his kind hazel eyes.

'Want to tell me what happened?' he said.

Tara's head whisked a fast 'no'. 'Nothing happened,' she said quietly. 'I just stumbled against my locker.' For a second she held her breath, convinced he would reply, 'But it wasn't your locker, was it?'

There was a pause.

'Okay, well, you'd better be off home then,' said Mr Ford. 'But if you need to talk then I'm —'

'I'm fine,' Tara said, relief blooming inside. 'Really. Thanks for sorting my arm out.'

She got up and hurried down the corridor. She could feel Mr Ford's gaze all the way to the main doors.

As soon as Tara got out of the school gates, she stopped and looked down at her opened fingers. The tiny treble clef was still there, squashed into her sweaty palm. She should have dropped it when she had the chance. Looking at the earring made her throat constrict and spots dance in front of her eyes. Tara looked around for a bin but there wasn't anywhere she could put it. It felt wrong to throw it on the ground. Sighing shakily, she stuffed it into the very furthest corner of the messenger bag she used for school.

Tara headed for the river to walk home. It was longer that way but she needed to clear her head before Mum saw her and sensed something was up.

The warm day had become muggy now and tiny flies

21

floated in clouds around her head. Tara's thoughts raced and flitted like the flies as she tried to take slow breaths and work out what had just happened.

The cold terror. The choking sense of panic. The desperate need to be found before something awful happened. For a few moments she'd been absolutely certain – as certain as her own name was Tara Elizabeth Murray – that Melodie Stone was in some kind of terrible danger.

There was only one time she'd felt like that before.

When Tyler Evans went missing.

But she'd been so wrong then. Horribly, disastrously wrong. She'd thought she was helping, and because of her a life was wasted.

Tara bit her lip and squeezed her hands into her eyes, making the world a kaleidoscope when she pulled them away.

Her insides lurched at the memory of her parents' faces. The way they'd avoided her eyes for days and said things like, 'Let's just try to forget all about this.'

But she knew she would never forget.

Tara tried to push the memories of February away. This wasn't going to happen. Melodie Stone had gone to live in Brighton. She was perfectly all right. It was nothing to do with Tara, and anyway, Tara's 'visions' weren't even to be trusted, not when it came to people.

She couldn't – wouldn't – put herself through that again.

She was going to be normal.

It didn't seem a lot to ask. She wasn't asking for fantastic hair or to be the most popular person in the school.

She just wanted to be normal.

CHAPTER 3

SHINY

Tara was watching morning television, her empty cereal bowl on the coffee table in front of her. She'd slept better than she expected to, and there had been no bad dreams. What had happened yesterday nagged at her now she was up though. It was taking all her mental energy to focus on the feature about fake tans on the telly. She looked at her phone, which was lying on the coffee table. Someone from an unknown number had tried to call her yesterday evening. *Probably a wrong number*, she thought.

Beck thumped down next to her and simultaneously crossed his legs on the table, his four slices of toast nearly skidding off his plate. His big, pale feet were almost obscuring the television. Tara smacked his leg.

'Urgh,' she said. 'Move your horrible hairy toes out of the way. I can't see.'

Beck lifted a leg so his foot dominated the screen and she shrieked and battered his leg with ineffectual slaps.

'Mum!' she yelled. 'Will you tell this hairy idiot to just stop!'

Mum came into the room, putting in one of her earrings.

'Stop, hairy idiot,' she deadpanned. 'Tara, it's time to go anyway. Come on.'

Tara got up and Beck instantly stretched along the sofa, thin white ankles and feet hanging off the end. Tara shot him a disgusted look and he grinned and folded a whole piece of toast into his mouth at once.

'God, you're foul,' she said and picked up her school bag, suppressing a tiny smile at the same time. 'How you ever got a girlfriend is one of life's mysteries.'

Beck just grinned again and reached for the remote control.

He was really called Jack, but Tara had called him Beck when she was a toddler and it had stuck. He seemed to sail through life in a way Tara deeply envied. She didn't sail. She felt as though she constantly got snagged on sharp things, like a kite caught in the branches of a tree.

Today was one of Mum's working days, so she gave Tara

a lift into school. Her mother had a frightening ability to know when something was wrong, so Tara tried to think of a topic of conversation to head her off at the pass. But she wasn't quite fast enough.

'Are you all right, Tabs?' said Mum, using the pet name she'd used since Tara was tiny. 'Only you didn't eat much of your dinner last night.'

'Yeah, I'm okay,' said Tara, flicking a bright smile and then looking straight ahead again.

'Really, really?' said Mum.

'Really, really.'

The car slowed and she felt her mum's glance grazing her cheek. She kept her face turned the other way.

'Is everything going okay at school?'

Tara sighed, inwardly. 'Yeah, it's all good,' she said.

'I know it's not easy settling into a new school,' continued Mum, 'but it'll come, you'll see.'

Her mother's soft, kind voice had the most annoying effect of making tears burn her eyes. She nodded briskly and grunted. When the car stopped at the side of the road, she got out without saying goodbye. She knew Mum would be hurt, but if she told her about last night and how, for a few horrible moments, she had been convinced that Melodie Stone was lost somehow and in danger, it would have sent her mother into the stratosphere with worry.

All the same, it didn't seem fair she should have to deal with this ... whatever it was ... alone.

The thing that really sucked was that Tara's freaky 'trick' used to make people happy. Lost your keys? Ask

Tara. Can't find where you left your wallet? Ask Tara.

It had started on the way back from a big shopping centre when Tara was two and a half. Tara had heard the story so many times, she fancied now that she remembered it all herself. As they'd driven home, Dad had noticed that his watch wasn't on his wrist. It was an expensive diving watch, which had been a special gift from his parents years before, and the strap had needed adjusting because one of the links was loose.

He had been trying on suits for an upcoming wedding in lots of different shops while Mum had taken Tara and Beck to get new shoes and ice creams. The shopping centre was huge and the watch worth a lot of money, so Dad was worried it was gone for good. They'd rushed back and Dad had started to ring the shops he'd visited but nothing had been handed in.

Tara had been whiney all the way home, repeating something over and over again and becoming increasingly agitated. She went into a full meltdown in the house and, finally, Mum realised she was trying to say something.

'Daddy wash in da shiny shop!'

The 'shiny shop' was the big department store, which had a striking display at the entrance of glass baubles that caught the light and sparkled like jewels.

There was a call from that very shop, minutes later. Dad's watch had been found underneath one of the displays.

Her parents had been delighted by their clever girl,

but no one could understand how she'd known. Tara had never been in the shop that day.

As she got older, Tara's gift for finding lost things was her party trick, even though it gave her a bit of a headache after it happened. No one minded it. It was just a bit of fun.

But it turned out that lost watches and keys were one thing, and lost little boys something else entirely.

Walking through the school gates that morning, past jostling, yelling younger kids and huddles of older ones talking, texting and laughing, Tara kept her head down. Maybe she could pretend the powerful sensations she'd felt by Melodie's locker meant nothing. If you forced yourself to believe something was true, maybe it became a kind of reality in time. That was what she was hoping, anyway.

The school day passed slowly. At breaktime, Tara noticed a battered old sports car near the school gates, its engine idling. She couldn't see the driver. Then she saw Karis from her form group looking around in a sneaky way before going over to the gates and letting herself out.

A man got out of the car. He looked familiar. Young, good-looking, with longish hair and a little beard. He wore skinny jeans and a T-shirt. She couldn't place where she'd seen him before. He started to talk to Karis, gesticulating and saying something in a heated way. After another brief exchange, he got back into the car and drove off.

Karis came back into school, eyes fervently darting around. Instead of going to find her cronies, Karis sat down on a bench, her back to some Year Sevens giggling on the other end.

'Oi!' The voice came from just outside the gate. Beck was grinning at Tara from outside, hands in his pockets. His jeans and the skin of his tanned arms were covered in splashes and flecks of white paint. She felt a rush of affection for her brother, who seemed like something warm and comforting in a hard, cold place.

'What are you doing here?' said Tara, walking over to the gate. She saw Karis's head whip up so fast she might crick her neck and a small tingle of pride went through her at her good-looking, funny brother, who everyone always liked. It sometimes felt as though all the charm and charisma had been handed out at once when Beck was born, leaving none for her when she came along, twenty months later.

'I'm on my way home,' he said, 'and I was passing because I had to drop something off down the road. Saw you standing there all alone and thought I'd say hello.'

'Oh, cheers.' Tara blushed, wishing Beck hadn't seen her looking like such a loser.

'You all right?' he said in an upbeat voice.

'Yeah, I'm good.' She straightened her spine and forced herself to smile.

'Good,' said Beck. 'Anyway, better go before I have to fight off packs of screaming girlies.' He grinned and Tara saw his gaze shift to the side. She turned to see Karis, who was smiling at Beck and sticking her chest out like some kind of overheated duck.

Tara sighed. 'Yeah, I wonder how you make it down the street sometimes,' she said drily.

'You said it, sister.' His stupid American accent made her laugh, despite herself. 'Anyway, people to see, lunch to be eaten. Later, Tar.'

He sauntered off. Tara turned to see Karis regarding her with an expression she hadn't seen from her before. It was a mixture of respect and envy.

Tara knew Karis wouldn't be able to help herself so she started to walk by as though she hadn't noticed her eager expression. It was a bit childish. But fun. She'd had a lot of practice in dealing with fans of her brother.

'Who's that then?' said Karis quickly, when she was almost past her.

Tara turned, a quizzical expression on her face as though she was miles away. 'Did you say something?'

Karis frowned and tipped her chin. 'Who was that?'

'Oh, that's my brother,' said Tara. She turned and, quick as a flash, Karis was next to her.

'He's almost eighteen and, yes, of course he's got a girlfriend, what did you think?' said Tara rapidly.

Karis's eyebrows shot upwards, then she gave Tara what looked suspiciously like a grin.

'Plus,' said Tara, feeling emboldened, 'haven't you already got someone?'

Karis looked confused. 'Eh?' she said. 'What d'you mean?'

Tara gestured to the gates with a nod of her head. 'Saw you with that bloke in the car a minute ago.'

Karis looked away. 'Ah, well, he's not mine. Unfortunately. He's Melodie's man, Will. He keeps hanging around, wanting to know if we've heard from her. He's being a bit of a pain, actually. He's a bit obsessed about it.'

Melodie's man? So who was Mr Mean And Moody by the river? Maybe he'd found out she was cheating on him with this Will. Maybe he'd done something to her in a fit of jealousy? Maybe Melodie was lying at the bottom of the river right now . . .

Tara shuddered. *Stop it, Tara. Don't do this.*

'So . . .' she forced herself to say, '*have* you heard from her then?'

Karis's eyes narrowed. 'Don't you start,' she said. 'And why do *you* care, anyway?'

'Just wondered,' said Tara. She felt as though she were digging a horrible, deep hole with every word, but only seemed to be able to burrow further. 'She's all right, then?'

'Of course she's all right. Why? Have you heard something?' Karis spoke sharply.

'No, I just wondered. You know, because she left so suddenly.' Tara's voice sounded strangled and weird to her own ears. 'Seemed a bit strange.'

Karis glanced across the piazza and Tara's eyes followed. Jada and Amber were watching them. Karis sighed.

'Well, I'm sure she's fine. It's just like her to leave

suddenly, if you ask me. And why wouldn't she be fine anyway?'

'No reason,' said Tara. Pins and needles buzzed in her fingers as she remembered the image from the day before. The single, naked lightbulb with its sickly glow. The stone floor. And then it was gone. She shivered and rubbed her arms, suddenly freezing.

The playground shimmered and wobbled. She was going to be sick. 'Gotta go.'

She ran to the girls' toilets and made it into a cubicle seconds before throwing up.

Afterwards, she gulped water from the tap and patted cold water all over her clammy face. Tara looked at herself in the mirror that was pocked with rust, feeling a thousand years old. Her green eyes looked bigger than normal in her pale face. Everybody kept saying Melodie was fine. As Karis said, why wouldn't she be fine?

And frankly, why should Tara even care? She didn't even like her.

She'd been wrong before anyway. A vivid memory of a weeping, distraught face flashed into her mind and something crumpled inside. Tears stabbed her eyes as the familiar feeling of hot shame washed over her. She scratched her arms, as if invisible bugs were working under her skin. It made her feel dirty sometimes, the guilt. Like she would never be able to wash it away.

'Beck?'

It was evening.

'Yeah?' Her brother's gaze didn't move from the screen. He tossed a chocolate peanut from the bag resting on the arm of the chair and effortlessly caught it between his teeth.

Tara was curled in the big chair with a blanket round her. A cup of camomile tea sat next to her on the coffee table. She'd told Mum she felt ill and her mother had gone into full clucky mode. She'd offered to miss Pilates but Tara said she'd be fine, even though for a moment she'd wanted to be small again, snuggled up with her mother on the sofa, watching CBeebies. It wasn't like she was ill. This churning inside wasn't to do with any bug or bad food. The urge to tell someone what had happened by that locker was gnawing at her but every time she tried to put the right words into any kind of order, they made no sense any more.

'Nothing,' she said wearily. 'Giz a peanut.'

Beck promptly threw one and it caught her squarely on the forehead – the missile not only painful, but sticky too.

'You git!' Tara leapt up and jumped on her brother. He was strong but she was quick and she caught him by surprise so she was able to stuff a cushion on his shoulders and sit on it before he could uncurl his long body.

There were muffled cries and then he grabbed her middle and spun her round so she was flat on the sofa. He lowered his bum towards her head. She screamed and battered at him with ineffectual hands. He calmly flicked through television channels with the remote while she squirmed beneath him.

'Say you submit, or I'll do it. You know I'll do it,' said Beck.

Tara shuddered. She knew what he was capable of in this situation. She forced her body to relax.

'I submit,' she said through gritted teeth.

'I submit, god-like deity.'

'*I submit, god-like deity!*'

He rolled away and she stumbled to her feet, hair all over the place and her face sweaty and hot.

'I hate you,' she said good-naturedly as she hurriedly got out of reach. 'And deity *means* god, moron, so you just said god-like god.'

Beck aimed another peanut at her. She yelped and scurried into the kitchen. She was smiling a little now. Or at least her face was marginally less rigid than it had been earlier. She craved familiarity tonight and wished Beck would somehow magically pick up on her need to talk. But as her brother generally had the empathy of an amoeba, this was a pointless wish.

He might not be one for deep and meaningful chats, but that didn't mean Beck didn't care. When everything had kicked off, Beck had never judged her or said anything critical, unlike everyone else in the world. That wasn't to say he hadn't looked out of his depth, and for once he hadn't had a joke or wind-up comment to hand. She'd caught him looking at her a few times and then smiling awkwardly, as though he didn't really know his little sis any more. That had almost been more painful than anything. But he knew she was hurting and that hurt him too.

She couldn't talk to him about this, though.

She couldn't talk to anyone.

Tara made herself more tea and went off into her bedroom. She sat down at her desk and looked around. Her new bedroom was much bigger than the old one, but it still felt wrong. Moving house had forced decisions about half the things she'd owned. She was too old to hang on to Furbies, Tamagotchis and ten-metre swimming certificates. But she hadn't really wanted to throw them away either.

Tara rested her elbows on the desk, her thick black hair swishing across her face. It fell into waves no matter how much she straightened it. She'd always longed to have blond, silky hair, despite Mum and Dad saying hers was lovely. Blond hair like Melodie's. An immediate mental picture of Melodie's hair caught in weeds at the bottom of the river popped into her mind. But it was only her imagination playing tricks, she knew that. The images had been so strong before. They were entirely different.

She gave a frustrated growl. She should leave it alone. If she started asking people about Melodie Stone, they would think she was mad. Or worse, had some kind of crush on her. She could just imagine the mileage the Gossip Girls would get from *that*. She actually shuddered at the thought.

The 'vision', or whatever it was, had felt so intense though. It felt like some knowledge was gnawing inside her; a rat with needle teeth that she couldn't ignore. Maybe she could just put her mind to rest. But how?

Tara stared at her noticeboard, not seeing it, thinking hard.

She needed proof that Melodie was safe, well and being a bitch somewhere else.

Tara huffed out air and her fringe rippled. She picked up a pen and tapped it on the desk, trying to think. Then she started to make notes on the pad in front of her, as she always did when her mind was unsettled.

Tell Mum?? She crossed this through so hard, the paper beaded in a tear.

Speak to Mr Ford?

She quickly crossed this through too. He'd look at her with those concerned eyes and be annoying about whether she was 'settling in'.

Ask Karis for Melodie's address?

Nope. Bad idea.

Find the boy she was cheating on?

Tara's pencil hovered over this and she started to doodle around the words. Maybe he really had done something to Melodie. Her heart lurched. You heard about stuff like that all the time in the news. Should she tell someone? But there wasn't anything to tell. And as far as the whole world was concerned, Melodie Stone was perfectly okay. It was just Tara who had the burning, horrible certainty that she had never been less okay. She was going to have to research this herself. And then maybe she would be free of it.

She concentrated hard on remembering what the boy looked like. She had a good memory. Sometimes too good. It made some things hard to forget.

Anyway, she could see him in her mind's eye: the dark eyes, the muscled arms and arrogant swagger. The T-shirt that clung in all the right places. Then she opened her eyes. The T-shirt had something written on the back.

Lifeguard.

It wasn't much to go on. But it was a start.

CHAPTER 4

LIFEGUARD

It was a half day for most of the school because of a careers event in the Sixth Form, so Tara had a free afternoon.

She stuffed a towel and the bikini she'd eventually found at the back of her knicker drawer into her school sports bag. They were only props. She had no intention of actually getting into the water.

When she'd got to the big leisure centre in town she was relieved to see a spectators' gallery above the Olympic-sized pool. Rows of plastic seats reached almost to the high ceiling, giving her a good vantage point to watch the pool.

It was loud and hot, the air heavy with chlorinated

moisture. Tara spent twenty minutes watching young children splashing about and adults joylessly totting up lengths. But there was no sign of the boy. Then she realised none of the lifeguards even wore a T-shirt like his. Instead, theirs were yellow with the leisure centre logo on them. Annoyed at herself for not realising this straight away, she got up to leave.

She bought a drink from the vending machine and sipped it, feeling flat about her wasted afternoon. It was all pointless anyway. Melodie bloody Stone. Instead of being here Tara could be . . .

. . . where, exactly?

She searched her mind for what she might be doing and, finding nothing, felt a sharp kick of loneliness.

Tara decided she might as well be thorough now she'd got this far. She wandered over to the information desk. A girl not much older than herself with blond hair extensions in a long, tight ponytail was texting, head down. Her long nails were painted silver with tiny black cats on them.

'Um, excuse me?' said Tara.

The girl's head shot up, her high ponytail bouncing. 'Yeah?'

'Is this the only pool around here?'

The girl nodded.

Tara sighed. 'Okay, thanks then.'

'Don't be silly, Jasmine. Have you forgotten about the lido?' An older woman bustled out from a door at the back with a stack of leaflets in her arms.

'Oh, yeah,' said the girl, Jasmine, making a disapproving face.

'Lido?' said Tara. 'What's that . . . like an outdoor one?'

'Yes,' the woman said with a smile. 'Lovely old place really. I learnt to swim there. Bit too cold for wimps these days though,' she said and batted the girl's arm with the leaflets.

'Urgh,' said Jasmine with feeling. 'Nasty old dump. Wouldn't catch me there.'

Tara thanked them and, armed with a map the older woman had given her, set off to walk across town to the lido.

Thick white cloud blanketed the sky, oppressive and low. She slipped in her earbuds and turned on her iPod, hoping to drown the sensible voice in her head. It kept saying things like, 'You're not going to find him,' and 'What would you even say, if you did? "Hello, have you kidnapped Melodie Stone?"'

She marched on through the centre of town and out past several large housing estates, before crossing the ring road and heading towards where she knew there was a large woodland area and park. This was where the woman had said the lido was located, although Tara hadn't remembered seeing it when she and her family had gone for a walk that way shortly after moving in.

She realised she'd walked round in a circle after a while and was close to giving up when she saw an entrance to the park across the road. Tara looked crossly at the crumpled map in her hand. She'd somehow missed the main entrance and walked almost to the top end of the park, adding to her journey. Her sandals were hurting now and her T-shirt clung with dampness to her back. It was warm, despite the heavy cloud. Everyone kept saying it was the warmest October in a hundred years.

Grumpily, she cut through a car park towards a large playground and sandpit. She asked a woman on a stand selling ice creams where the lido was and the woman pointed to a large white structure in the distance. She would have seen it straight away if she'd come in at the right gate. She thanked the woman and wolfed down an ice lolly to ease her parched throat.

The lido was an ugly sort of building with two columns bordering the entrance that looked as though they had been stuck on as an afterthought.

An elderly man in a greasy baseball cap was sitting in a booth just inside the gates. He had large ears with long lobes that dangled like fleshy earrings.

Tara could make out a long slice of aquamarine just beyond where he sat. She felt a sharp kick of longing to feel cool water on her hot and dusty skin.

'How much for a swim?' she said. The old man eyed her suspiciously, even though she appeared to be his only customer. He spent a moment sorting something under the desk and then produced a small rubber stamp.

'Three pound, lockers fifty pence non-returnable,' he said like a robot, unsmiling. 'Hand.'

'Pardon?'

'Give us your hand.'

Tara held out her hand cautiously and the old man grasped it in his own clammy one before stamping it with a blurry picture of a seahorse.

She swallowed a strong urge to giggle. 'Won't that wash straight off?'

The old man shrugged and turned back to the newspaper spread out on the shelf below the main desk, which was open at a crossword. A chewed-looking biro lay on the top next to a pack of rolling tobacco and a stained, chipped coffee mug.

The man started to investigate an ear with his little finger, face turned down again. Tara grimaced and quickly passed through the turnstile to the pool area. The blast of chlorine here was even stronger than at the leisure centre. A few brown leaves lay on the top of the water. A girl in her twenties, wearing a T-shirt and shorts, was fishing what looked like a crisp packet out of the pool with a long net. She gave Tara a nod. The only person in the pool was an old woman in a yellow swimming hat covered in huge rubber daisies. Nut brown, she bobbed along like a cork, covering barely any distance.

There was no sign of the boy. Tara heaved a sigh. She'd walked miles, getting all sweaty and blistered for a stupid wild goose chase. Maybe he just liked that T-shirt. It didn't mean it had his job description on it. Didn't Beck have one that said *Gangsta*, after all?

She looked down at the blue rippling water. Despite the crisp packet and the splodges of brown leaves, it lapped invitingly against the tiles, looking cool and refreshing. The tiles were cracked and faded, but featured a blue and green mosaic, with a simple representation of a fish drawn in two sweeping movements. The image was repeated in every second tile. It must have been quite pretty once. Tara had to admit it was nicer than the leisure centre. That woman had been right, even if it was all a bit cruddy and old.

Tara jumped when a screeching feedback sound assaulted her ears. There was a high-pitched screech and then tinny music floated over the pool. It was some cheesy old Eighties track her dad liked. Maybe the bloke taking tickets felt two swimmers warranted a bit of background music, she thought. But she hadn't even decided if she was going in yet.

The changing rooms were a series of poolside cubicles with doors that didn't meet the ceiling or floor. Tara chewed her lip, thinking. It wasn't a very private place to get changed.

She was very hot though . . .

Making a snap decision, Tara stepped into a cubicle at the far end of the pool, which smelt of bleach with something sour underneath it. The floor was dirty and wet. Tara carefully undressed in the small space, standing on top of her sandals to avoid touching the floor for as long as possible.

She didn't have anything to tie her hair back with, which was annoying, so she tried to plait it roughly and twist it into a knot. She wished she'd brought her stout Speedo swimsuit instead of this bikini, which was white with tiny roses all over it. She'd bought it specially for the pool party where things first happened with Jay last year. She should have thrown it away. Maybe the memory of his approving eyes grazing up and down her body had stopped her, even though it felt like a fist was reaching into her chest and squeezing her heart painfully to think of it. Anyway, she'd never really intended to put it on today. Even the towel she'd tugged from the airing cupboard wasn't really big enough for practical drying purposes.

Yet despite all this, a few minutes later, she emerged from the changing room and thrust her clothes into the nearest locker. She had to deposit the fifty-pence coin several times before it clanged noisily into place.

Despite being a strong swimmer, Tara wasn't a diver so much as a careful stepper-in when it came to cold water. Leaving her sandals right at the pool's edge, she climbed slowly down the ladder, gasping with shock as the water crept up over her knees and then her thighs. It was so much colder than she'd expected – a burning iciness that was more extreme than any pool she'd ever been in before. More like seawater. For a second she fancied she caught a briny smell on a breeze that drew the hairs on her arms up, even though they were miles from the coast.

Tentatively, she lowered her shoulders under the water, shuddering from her toes upwards at the zinging shock engulfing her.

She swam off, slowly at first, and then warmth flooded her limbs. She sliced strong strokes through the water. It had been years since she'd done this but muscle memory kicked in, guiding her effortlessly. She'd loved swimming once. But when she got to Year Six, self-consciousness about showing her body had taken over. She hadn't stepped into a swimming pool for years, right up until the day when she'd gone to that pool party . . .

Sadness welled up inside at the memory of Jay's closed eyes as he'd come in to kiss her. The heat of his mouth by her ear whispering, 'You're all I want. No one else.'

Oh, get out of my head, you loser, she thought.

Tara stopped by the side of the pool, holding on to the rough edge for a moment, then took a breath and plunged downwards. Bubbles spiralled from her body as she went down.

Grasping the ladder that reached to the bottom of the pool, she wedged her feet at the bottom and clung on, resisting the powerful pull that tried to bring her back to the surface.

When she was younger, she used to lie on the bottom of the bathtub and count as high as she could before her screaming lungs forced her upwards. The splash used to soak the bathroom floor and annoyed her mother no end. Her record had been one minute and thirty seconds.

But now, her lungs cramped quickly. The pain overrode the ache of thinking about everything and brought a masochistic sort of relief.

She stubbornly held on, counting twenty, then thirty, then forty seconds, all the while fighting the pull of the water, which was trying to throw her back to the surface like an unwanted mermaid. The feeling of control was good. She couldn't control much in her life, especially the guilt that ate her like a cancer inside. But she could fight this with her lungs and her will.

Opening her eyes, she let the stinging water flood into them, welcoming the discomfort. Her hair had come undone and floated around her head like dark weeds.

But there was something there. A dark shape wobbled above her. A face. Someone was leaning over.

To hold her under.

CHAPTER 5

GODS

Erupting through the water like an arrow, Tara swallowed water that scorched her throat and nostrils. Gasping, she struggled to breathe.

'Hey, it's all right!' said a male voice, loud and startled. 'I didn't mean to scare you!'

As her vision cleared, she realised it was a boy.

No, it was *the* boy.

He was crouched down at the side of the pool, dressed in the same T-shirt and shorts as the other lifeguard. He had a pair of flip-flops on his tanned feet. His expression was shocked, his eyes wide.

'I shouted for ages but you didn't hear me!' he said,

looking horrified.

Tara gulped air into her tight lungs. She rubbed water from her face, wishing she could just make a hole in the side of the pool and swim away. She looked around. There was no one else here now and the sky was filled with tumbling clouds in shades of silver and black.

'What do you want?' she managed to squeak.

'You have to get out of the pool,' he said, bouncing on his calves and standing up in one fluid movement. 'There's a thunderstorm coming. It's not safe to swim in a storm. Thought I was going to have to jump in and get you.'

'Oh,' said Tara tightly. 'Okay.'

He walked away and started to pull grey sheets of tarpaulin over grubby-looking plastic sun loungers which were speckled with insect bodies. Tara climbed out of the pool, self-consciously rearranging her bikini bottoms as soon as she had a hand free. Not that he or anyone else was looking at her. Not that there was anyone else *but* him.

She scurried past the boy and collected her stuff from the locker, shivering all over. The air felt charged and her skin sang with it. She was freezing. She knew she looked awful, with her hair plastered to her skull. And she'd just made a total muppet of herself. But despite all this, she felt energised. Better, in fact, than she had for ages.

It really was a stupidly small towel that she'd brought with her though, she thought as she tried to dry herself with ineffectual dabs. Teeth chattering now, she ended up pulling on her T-shirt over damp skin. Her cut-off jeans seemed to sandpaper her mottled, goose-bumpy thighs as she dragged them on.

The crack of thunder made her flinch. He'd been right to get her out, even if he *had* given her a fright.

By the time she came out of the cubicle, trying to drag her fingers through tangled, wet hair that clung miserably to her neck, the rain was falling in javelins, bringing a smell of earth and metal so rich her nose almost twitched with it. It felt like the world was being woken up from the heavy, drowsy warmth of earlier, literally electrified into life.

The boy was waiting inside the entrance with his back to her, a heavy set of keys in his hand. He tapped them against his leg as if in rhythm to music playing in his head. Tara noticed how his strong shoulders and back sloped in a V to his narrow waist. He had long legs, in jeans now, and the flip-flops had been replaced by black and red trainers. He turned to her, his face impassive, and then quickly looked away.

'I'm supposed to lock up,' he said gruffly, 'but you can hang about if you like, until this lets up. I'm not going anywhere in that lot.'

'Thanks,' said Tara, glad she didn't have to step into the rain. It was drumming down so hard that it splashed back up, as though reversing its journey. The opportunity to talk to the boy had been handed to her so easily, but she couldn't think what to say. The very idea of playing detective was about as appealing as doing a naked dance in the rain.

And he wasn't exactly Mr Chatty. It seemed unlikely he would be the one to begin a conversation. They stood there in silence for several minutes. There was no let up in the rain. Over by the car park, Tara could see a man sheltering under a tree with his hood up.

Eventually, the boy spoke.

'Do I know you?' he said, eyes slightly narrowed, as he looked at her.

'I, uh . . .'

Tara's ability to speak had been snatched away as though by some malign magic. Did he recognise her from the riverbank? She prayed he didn't.

The boy's gaze took in her sports bag.

'Oh, you go to Foxton Heath,' he said. 'You probably know my sister, Mel Stone? Melodie?'

Tara's insides looped the loop. She suppressed a mad urge to laugh triumphantly at this conversational gift.

'Yeah, we're really good mates.' The lie flew out of her mouth before her rational mind could stop it. He definitely didn't remember meeting her on the river path; that was clear.

So this was Melodie's *brother*. They couldn't have looked more different; she was blond, and he was dark and Mediterranean-looking.

'I'm Leo,' he said. She forced a knowing look, as though she'd heard about him, many times before. He had a quiet speaking voice and Tara had to listen hard to be able to hear his words.

'Tara,' she said, heart thumping almost painfully hard

in her chest. For a split second she'd almost lied and said 'Karis'. She was glad she resisted. He'd be bound to know Melodie's real friends.

Leo frowned. It was obvious he was trying to remember his sister mentioning her. Tara's breath caught. She was useless at lying, but Leo didn't seem to have picked up on anything. 'Was sure I'd seen you before,' he said.

You have, thought Tara. *Just not in the way you think you have.*

Seizing on the advantage, she said, 'How's it going in Brighton then?' even though her face was starting to heat up, treacherously. Of the many things she hated about herself, her tendency to blush at the wrong times was high on the list. Her dad was Scottish and joked that his nation went from blue to white in the sun. Tara's delicate pale skin stained crimson at the slightest provocation. Dad called her his 'apple-cheeked beauty', which didn't help a whole lot.

But Leo wasn't looking at her. He stared ahead and sighed deeply. 'Dunno,' he said. 'Good, I expect. We're not exactly . . .' He bit the rest of the sentence back and looked away. 'She's probably having a great time. She usually gets the best out of situations, does our Mel.'

Tara forced herself to stay silent, hoping he would say more.

Leo glanced at her. 'You don't seem like her usual sort of friend,' he said after a moment.

Indignation blasted through her like hot air. 'Why? What's wrong with me?' she said.

'Nothing – I mean, you're …' Leo was blushing too now.

'What?' Was he going to actually tell her to her face that she wasn't good enough to hang out with Melodie poxy Stone? Why had she even come here today?

'Well …' Leo took an audible in-breath. '… they all seem a bit … shallow. Can't imagine any of them having a swim. You know, in case it messed up their hair.'

'Oh.' It felt like a compliment wrapped up in an insult and she wasn't sure exactly how she should respond. Was he saying she didn't care about how she looked? Or that she wasn't a vain airhead? Could he mean both those things at once? This whole conversation was hard work.

Silence fell between them.

The rain was beginning to ease up a little. The trees ahead were blurred around the edges, like in a watercolour painting. The air was laden with fine moisture. The greenery of the park was so emerald-intense it almost hurt to look at. The figure in the car park had gone.

'I'd better lock up now,' said Leo, quietly, 'or Dobby'll kick off.'

Remembering the old man who'd taken her money on the way in, Tara couldn't help the laugh that rippled up her cheeks. 'Dobby? Because of …?' She touched her ears, grinning.

Leo frowned. 'No, his name is Mr Dobby,' he said, poker-faced.

Tara's facial heating system went critical. Then she saw a twinkle in Leo's eye. A slight grin crinkled the corner of his mouth.

'Had you for a moment, didn't I?' he said. 'Come on, we'd better get out of here before he comes and gives me a gnome bite or something.'

Tara murmured her response.

'What was that?' said Leo, as she stepped outside.

'Dobby's a house-elf, not a gnome.' *Oh God, shut up Tara, you stupid, geeky idiot . . .*

But Leo's eyes were warm as he regarded her.

'Yeah. Course he is.'

As she reached the car park, Tara looked back and saw Leo folding his tall frame into a small white car.

Her heel still hurt and her damp hair felt horrible, but she was hungrier than she could remember being in ages. Even though her limbs were heavy from the swim, she felt buzzy and good too. She turned the conversation with Leo over in her mind. He was a weird mixture of gruff and kind of gentle. Could it be that despite the way he looked, he was shy? Tara found it hard to imagine that someone that good-looking could ever be shy. What did he have to be shy about? Although, admittedly, she was a bit shy herself and her parents were always telling her she was pretty. But then, they were her parents and bigging up their offspring was in their job description.

Jay had told her she was pretty too. But Jay had been a liar in so many ways, she'd stopped counting.

She was pretty sure Leo didn't seem like someone who would have bumped off his sister. She'd made an enquiry like a proper little detective and maybe now she could leave it alone. At least she'd had a good swim. And even with the dodgy changing rooms and the grubby floor, the complete lack of water heating and the scowling house-elf who took the money, the lido did . . . have its own attractions. Maybe she'd go back. Just to get a bit fitter.

As she crossed the main road outside the park, she had the strangest sensation of being watched. But why would anyone? Anyway, when she looked, no one was there.

She was starving now and started picturing a big slice of crusty bread with thick yellow butter on the top, washed down with a cold glass of juice. Her mouth watered at the vivid image.

And then from nowhere, footsteps pounded behind her.

She turned and cried out, all instincts telling her to attack or run. But she was frozen to the spot in shock. There was a man there, looking a little out of breath. He touched her arm lightly.

'Hey, I didn't mean to scare you!' It was the second time today someone had said this to her.

Tara realised she was looking at the man – boy, really – who had been hovering outside the school talking to Karis. Melodie's boyfriend. Will. His eyes were big, shocked, like he was the one who'd had the fright. He backed away, hands upwards.

'I'm sorry, I just wanted to talk to you!'

Tara tried to calm her breath, which was coming in rapid, panicked bursts.

'What do you want?' she said, taking a step back on

54

legs so wobbly her knees almost buckled.

In a rush, Tara remembered why he'd looked familiar when she saw him the last time. He was the boy in the photo booth picture in Melodie's locker. He was much younger than she'd previously thought, very early twenties at the most. But he was unshaven and his eyes were bloodshot. His breath smelt sour and the blue cotton shirt he was wearing was creased, with dark patches at the armpits. Despite all this, Tara could see he was good-looking in a loves-himself way. He had on skinny jeans and his shirt was open a little at the neck. A silver cross nestled in his dark chest hair. His hair was long around his collar and he had a tiny beard with girlish soft lips. His brown eyes were fringed with long lashes and it was possible he had a little bit of eyeliner on too. A leather satchel was slung across his shoulder.

He stepped back a little further. Tara tried to think quickly if anything in her bag could be used as a weapon and slipped her hand inside.

'Please,' he said, 'don't be frightened of me. I only want to talk to you, that's all.'

'Why?' snapped Tara, reaching into her bag. There was a deodorant spray in there. She could spray it in his eyes, perhaps. 'How do you even know me?'

The man ran a hand over his thick dark hair, which was greasy at the roots.

'I saw you talking to Leo at the pool,' he said, with a pleading sort of expression. 'He won't talk to me . . . but I thought you might.'

Alarm leapt in her throat again. She remembered the figure she'd seen earlier in the rain. 'Have you been following me?'

'Yes,' he said, and she gasped at his honesty. Then he added hurriedly, 'I was trying to pluck up courage to talk to Leo again but then I saw you and noticed your bag and . . . thought you might be able to help.'

'Help with what?' said Tara stiffly, pulling the bag across her front, like a shield.

'I only wanted to ask if you've heard from her, that's all!' His shoulders sagged. 'I've asked all her friends, but no one seems to be able to tell me anything.'

'What's to tell?' said Tara warily, but her hand was already moving away from the deodorant. There was nothing threatening about him now she'd got over the shock, not really.

He glanced around. 'Look, I know you have no reason to trust me and you don't know me, but can I get you a coffee or something? Just so we can talk?'

Tara regarded him. For all she knew, he could be some kind of rapist or axe murderer. But she didn't have enough money left to buy anything to eat. And she was curious to know why he was worried about Melodie. Her curiosity – along with hunger and thirst – won over reticence and she nodded hesitantly.

'All right then,' she said. 'But I haven't got very long.'

There was a café across the road called the Blue Cuckoo. The walls were hung with mirrors of all shapes and sizes and wooden painted birds hung on strings from the ceiling. Folk music played quietly in the background and the air was rich with coffee. The man bought two large doughnuts without asking her and brought over a glass of juice, which Tara had requested. Her mouth watered at the thought of the doughnut but she watched his every move as he handled her drink, in case he tried to slip something into it. She'd read about that too.

His hands trembled as he lifted his own espresso. He didn't look like a man who needed caffeine. He practically hummed with nervous energy. His eyes met with Tara's.

'I'm Will,' he said, searching her face. 'Mel's boyfriend.'

Tara took a bite of the doughnut to avoid having to answer. She chewed it and then swallowed before taking a sip of the orange juice. Her energy levels started to rise again.

'Aren't you a bit old for her?' she said.

Will looked affronted. 'I'm only twenty,' he said.

'Yeah, and she's fifteen,' said Tara, wishing she didn't sound so much like her mum.

'Age is an artificial construct,' said Will haughtily. 'It means nothing when you're in love. Why does everyone think this is such a big deal?'

'Whatever,' said Tara. 'Look, what do you want?'

He lowered his eyes and fiddled with the small cup in front of him with long slender fingers.

'I just want to know that she's okay, that's all,' he said. 'I've tried calling her, but it doesn't ring. I must have sent twenty emails but there's no reply.' He sat back in his seat. 'Something's not right. I haven't been able to sleep. And anyway, look what I found yesterday.'

Will reached into his bag and put down a small leather purse on the table. It was bright turquoise in colour with a felt owl stitched on the front. A sparkly M charm on a chain was attached to the zip.

'It's her purse,' said Will with a triumphant air. 'It was underneath a load of stuff in my room. My ma found it.' He had the grace to look a little sheepish at this admission.

'She's got bank cards and her student travelcard in there,' he continued. 'Why would she go to Brighton without those?'

That *was* odd, Tara had to privately admit. She thought about the bad feeling she'd had before and tried to shrug it away. None of this was her problem.

'Well . . . what do you think's happened to her?' she said, despite herself.

'I don't know,' said Will, shaking his head. 'I just don't buy that she's gone to live with her dad. She almost never sees him. To suddenly go and set up home in the rock-star palace now? Well, it doesn't add up.'

Will seemed to read the question in Tara's face.

'You know who her dad *is*, don't you?'

'No,' said Tara. 'I don't really even know *her*.' In fact, she was starting to wish she'd never even heard of Melodie Stone.

Will's expression sagged a little. 'Oh. I was hoping you did.' He took a sip of his coffee and sighed. 'Her dad's Adam Stone.' Tara made a puzzled face. 'Adam Stone from The Tin Gods?' he said.

'Oh . . .' Tara's eyes widened.

Everyone knew The Tin Gods. They were part of the whole Britpop thing in the early nineties. Tara's mum danced with embarrassing abandon if their music ever came on at parties. Their biggest hit, 'Best Days of Our Lives', was still played on the telly all the time. 'I didn't know.'

'She doesn't see him very often,' said Will balefully. 'He's got a new family and lives in some mansion in Brighton. He's reinvented himself as a food and wine buff and he's developed a couple of apps to do with restaurants. He's properly minted.'

'You seem to know a lot about him,' said Tara.

Will's face hardened. 'Hmm,' he grunted grumpily. 'Thought at one point he might be able to help me out, but he's obviously forgotten what being a struggling young musician is like.'

Ah . . . thought Tara. Seemed Will had reasons for disliking Adam Stone that had nothing to do with Melodie. Will had such a pouty sulk on his face now that Tara almost wanted to laugh.

'Like that, is it?' she said, draining the last of her juice.

Will widened his big brown eyes. 'No,' he said. 'I might not like the man, but I still don't believe Mel would go and live with him.' He paused. 'God!' He ran a hand over his beard. 'I've been there to mop up her tears when he's rejected her before. I don't buy that suddenly he's the loving father.'

Tara sighed. 'Look, none of this has anything to do

with me. I saw you talking to Karis the other day at school. What does she say?'

'She doesn't know anything. And that Jada is all huffy about it, like Mel's gone away just to upset them.'

'Been to the police?' Tara said, knowing it sounded lame.

Will raised an eyebrow, rather impressively. 'And say what? My underage girlfriend isn't answering my calls?'

Tara made a face. He made it sound really sleazy, put like that.

'Well, I don't see what I can do,' she said. Her earlier exertions were catching up with her. She felt tired and wanted to go home.

Will sat forward, his expression earnest. 'Look, you seem like a nice girl . . .' he began.

Patronise me a bit more, why don't you? thought Tara.

'Will you just do one thing for me?' he said. 'Then I'll leave you alone once and for all. If you'll just take the purse to Mel's house.' He reached into the leather satchel and produced a piece of paper. An address was written in flamboyant, curly handwriting. 'Say you found the purse under the bed or something at your house. There's a note from me in there. A message.'

Tara hesitated. 'Why don't you take it yourself?' she said.

Will took on a hunted, resentful look. 'Because of Faith's bloke, Ross. He threatened me the last time I went over there. Said if I didn't stop hanging around, he'd . . . well, it wasn't very nice, what he said. And I've been over there twice already. Like I said, this has only just turned up.'

'Post it then,' said Tara in exasperation.

'I don't trust them not to look through it and find my note, if it comes by post,' said Will in an annoyingly patient tone, as though he were speaking to someone very young or very stupid. 'They won't do that if *you* deliver it.'

'Who's Faith?' said Tara.

'Mel's aunt,' said Will. 'Her ma died when she was a baby and Faith had always lived with them, so she became Mel's guardian. Adam didn't want her.'

For the first time ever Tara felt a stab of sympathy for Melodie Stone.

'Give it here,' she said.

Will passed the purse across the table with an attractive, wide grin. Tara scooped the purse into her bag so she only touched it for a second, remembering the events of the other day. The memory brought a stab of alarm again.

'I don't know why I'm doing this,' she said grumpily. 'I don't even like the girl.' Saying these words to Melodie's biggest fan gave her a thrill of spiteful pleasure.

Will's face tightened. 'I know she can be high maintenance, but she hasn't had it easy. Faith ... well, she can be difficult. Her and Mel fight like cat and dog. And Ross is a right creep. Melodie can't stand him.' He paused. 'Look, if you'll just do this one thing for me, I'd be so grateful.' His soft eyes were all misty now. Tara hoped fervently that he wouldn't start crying.

She pushed back her chair and stood up. 'I said okay, didn't I?' she said.

Will's face relaxed into a smile and Tara could see why some girls might find him fanciable, what with the puppy-dog eyes and the white teeth, which he flashed at her now.

'That's fantastic,' he said. 'You're a real star. Here.' He pulled out a business card from the front of his satchel. 'If you could drop me a quick text when you've done it.'

Tara took the business card and piece of paper wearily, and glanced at the address. 'Fine,' she said. 'So where is this anyway? I'm not trekking miles to her house.'

'It's not too far,' he said hurriedly. 'It overlooks the river. You know where the old iron bridge is? The fancy one? It's right by there.'

Tara did know, unfortunately. It was where she had last seen Melodie.

'Well,' said Tara, 'thanks for the drink and the doughnut. I have to go now.'

She turned away, slipping his business card into her pocket.

CHAPTER 6

ANGEL

'You went *swimming*?' Mum appeared to find Tara's explanation for her afternoon out baffling, despite the wet bikini and towel coiled snail-like in the plastic bag in her hand. What with the stringy damp hair and the flushed cheeks, it ought to be proof enough, Tara thought.

'Why are you so surprised?' she said grumpily, decanting the wet things into the washing machine, her nose wrinkling at the sharp chlorine smell. 'I'm not some couch potato who never does anything.'

Her mother was vigorously mixing vegetables and chicken in the wok. She brushed a strand of her hair, as inky black as Tara's, but now kept that way by the hairdresser.

'Well,' said her mother, 'it's not that I'm surprised . . . Okay, I *am* surprised. It's just because you didn't mention it. But I think it's great. You used to be a right little fish when you were little.'

Tara involuntarily glanced at a photo on the bookcase. It showed her at ten, all fresh-faced and beaming as she held up a medal from a swimming gala. 'Yeah, guess I was,' she said absent-mindedly. It was all such a long time ago.

'So who did you go with?' said Mum, her voice glass-bright.

Tara sighed as she filled a glass of water from the tap. Her parents were obsessed with her making friends since they'd moved here. They couldn't seem to understand that their constant questions about school and who she sat next to and what 'the other girls' were like only served to make the feeling of having failed ten times worse.

'I went on my own, Mum,' said Tara wearily and walked towards the doorway.

'Tabs?'

She turned back. Mum was holding a wooden spoon in the air like she was conducting an orchestra with it. Her hair was even wilder than usual from the steamy kitchen air. Tara felt a rush of love, despite her irritation.

'What?' she said softly.

'You deserve better than Jay,' she said. 'You'll look back and wonder what you saw in the little creep one day.

Don't sell yourself short. Any boy should thank his lucky stars to have someone like you.'

Tara blinked, surprised. Mum obviously knew that Jay had been on her mind a lot. But in fact, Jay Burns hadn't entered her thoughts for hours now.

'Yeah,' she said with a smile, 'too right.'

Later, Mum had gone off to her monthly book group meeting and Dad was working late again. Tara curled up on the big chair with her laptop. Beck was having one of his ridiculously long showers. Mum always said he was way worse than any girl with his 'ablutions'. When he came out it took hours for the steam and aftershave smell to melt away.

Tara was looking at Google images of The Tin Gods, particularly Adam Stone. Most of the images were old, showing the bass guitarist in his early twenties, when he'd been thin and moody-looking, with a mop of fair curls. A recent image from a fund-raising gig for the charity Water Aid showed a portly, balding man with a ruddy face, and a glamorous, bony woman with a frosty smile on his arm. He had exactly the same shape eyes as Melodie.

Tara was almost disappointed by the realisation that Will had been right about Melodie's dad. She'd half hoped this had been a misguided fantasy. That way, it would be easier to ignore his obvious worries. For a moment she imagined what it must feel like to lose your mum when you were a baby and to know your dad didn't want you. A pang of sadness tugged her heart. Then she remembered how horrible Melodie was. Having bad things happen to you was no excuse for treating people like dirt. Tara had experienced bad things too, after all.

She sat back, the laptop balancing on the arm of the chair, and stared into the middle distance. It was odd that Melodie would leave her purse behind, though. But if something had happened, wouldn't it have been reported by now?

Tara was still deep in thought when Beck came into the room, a big towel wrapped round his waist, steam wafting around him, and his hair hedgehogged into spikes.

'Ah, crap,' he said and slapped his hand against the table. 'Left my phone at work, didn't I?'

'No, you didn't,' said Tara, distractedly. 'It's slipped down behind your bed. One of Sara's earrings is there too.' Sara was Beck's current girlfriend. The picture was as clear as if it had appeared on their new HDTV. And then it was gone.

Tara twiddled a strand of hair around her finger in a black spiral, debating whether she really was going to do what she'd promised Will. It took her a few seconds to register the change in the room. There was a weird stillness, but something unspoken charged the air. She looked up, her stomach swooping as she clocked the expression on her brother's face. He was staring at her, a wary half-smile on his lips.

He hurried out of the room. Tara heard him going

into his bedroom and the scrape of the bed being shifted against the wooden floorboards.

Oh no, she thought. *Stupid, stupid Tara. Why did I have to open my mouth?*

Beck came back into the room holding his iPhone. He had a glass drop earring in the other hand. He looked down at both items with a frown.

'Look,' Tara said, ' I —'

She had been about to make up an excuse but couldn't think of why she would be looking down the side of her big brother's bed. Beck sat down heavily on the sofa opposite her, his muscled shoulders still covered in drops of water, his face serious for once.

'It's still happening, isn't it?' he said. 'The whole spooky finding-stuff trick?'

Tara kept her eyes cast down. Tears were rising dangerously inside her. She nodded quickly, once, not trusting herself to speak.

'Tar?' Her brother's voice was low and gentle. 'Look at me, okay?'

She dragged her gaze up to meet his. Her eyes were now glittering and wet.

'It's okay,' said Beck gently. 'It'll be our little secret, yeah? No need for the olds to know, is there?' There was a long pause. 'Look,' he continued, 'I know it was rough on you, what happened back there, but it was really bad for Mum and Dad too.'

'I know that,' said Tara thickly, swallowing hard.

'But do you know *all* of it, though?' said Beck. 'How bad

it got? About how they only just avoided criminal charges?'

Tara sucked in her breath. She shook her head, speechless for a moment.

Beck's expression softened. 'They wanted it kept quiet. I only found out by accident,' he said gently. 'Anyway, Dad managed to talk the police out of it. The boy's mum . . . well, she would have had you hanged, drawn and quartered. If it was up to her, we'd probably all be banged up. Not to mention how the boy's dad kicked off. It was really embarrassing for the police.'

'You don't have to tell me that,' snapped Tara. She grabbed one of the cushions and squashed it against her damp face. She said something that was lost in the satin fabric.

'What?' said Beck. 'I can't hear you, because you have a cushion stuck to your face.'

Tara flopped back in the seat, the cushion in her lap. 'I *said*, I can't help it. It's not like I chose to be a weirdo. I'm not even a weirdo who gets it right.'

'Yeah,' said Beck with a smile. 'But you're *our* weirdo, eh?'

Tara shot her brother a disgusted look and then lobbed the cushion, which he caught with one hand.

'All I'm saying is let's keep this under the radar, yeah?' He paused. 'Oh and cheers. Sara was really upset about that earring.'

Tara nodded. Her brother got up, wafting Lynx. But when he reached the door he turned back, his face serious again.

'It's only phones and stuff, though?' he said.

Tara breathed slowly in through her nose and out through her mouth as he spoke.

There was a pause. 'Tar?'

'Yeah,' she said, avoiding his eye. 'Only phones and stuff.'

She went through to her bedroom and closed the door, before gently turning the key in the lock. For a moment she lay her forehead against the smooth wood, hearing Beck whistling in his room. No doubt his thoughts were already about Sara's gratitude later or whether Arsenal would get through to the next round of the Cup. How lucky he was. He had no idea what it was like being her.

A freak. And one step short of a murderer to boot.

She knew what she had to do when she felt like this.

Her hands were shaking as she opened her wardrobe. She reached to the very back of the shelf at the top. Rooting under the tangle of jumpers, her fingers finally found the cool metal lid of the biscuit tin.

Taking it carefully over to the bed, she stared down at it. A familiar nauseous heat seeped through her. She had been trying hard not to look in here recently. She'd even contemplated getting rid of the box and its painful contents a few weeks ago. She'd reasoned there was no point in keeping it. She knew what Mum would say. That it was morbid. And didn't people deserve a second chance, sometimes?

Maybe not Tara though. And forcing herself to look in the box reminded her all over again. It hurt. And the pain was what she needed and deserved.

Tara opened the lid and shook the contents onto the bed.

A few newspaper cuttings fell out, along with a letter handwritten on thin, lined paper. The paper was bruised with angry pressure points so it almost felt like braille. Tara imagined the pen pressing the savage words into it and the hate that flowed through them.

She couldn't look at that first. She always started with the newspaper cuttings. It was important that she did it in the right order. The first one was from the local newspaper in her old town, dated February this year.

MISSING!

A three-year-old Southam toddler has not been seen since playing in his garden on Tuesday. Tyler Evans is described by mother Siobhan as a 'bright, bubbly boy who we all love to bits'. If you have any information, please call.

There was another cutting, dated the following week.

TRAGIC TOT FIGHTS FOR LIFE

Brave Tyler Evans is said to be in a critical condition after being found near a railway track on Saturday.

The three-year-old was the subject of a countywide search after going missing for four days and was believed to have been abducted by Sean

Stanley, an ex-boyfriend of his mother Siobhan.

It is now thought the toddler wandered off and fell down the steep railway bank, sustaining serious injuries. Police claim the area had already been searched and have been heavily criticised for not finding the boy sooner.

Stanley is suing the force for damage to his home and injuries sustained during his arrest. Local MP Giles Meadows has called for an inquiry into what he described as a 'pig's ear of an investigation'.

And then ...

R.I.P. TYLER:
BRAVE TOT LOSES BATTLE FOR LIFE

Tara's eyes filled with hot tears. The words wobbled and blurred and her sinuses burned and fizzed. She dropped the cutting and reached for a tissue, before blowing her nose with a loud honk.

Hand trembling, she left the cutting where it was and took a long shaky breath before reaching for the letter. The paper had been thin and cheap to begin with, but Tara's countless handlings of it since February had given it the quality of something much older than it was too. Mum and Dad didn't know anything about her cuttings. The letter had been lying on the mat when she'd come home from school, addressed to *Tara Murry*. Still in a state of shock and moving through the world like a ghost, she'd opened it without any sense of what might be inside.

Tara smoothed out the pages and made herself read. The handwriting was childish and blocky.

Tara

I want you to understand what it is youve done to my family. If you hadnt gone to the police with your crap stories, my baby would still be alive. The police are to blame, I know, but YOU was the one that persauded them he was with his dad.

I cry all the time and the doctors had to give me pills. Chelsea and Jayden miss their brother and have nightmares every night. Our lives are in peaces and you are probably carrying on like nothing happened, tucked up in your nice house with your mum and dad. I know you have a brother. How would you feel if he was dead?

I hope you have nightmares too Tara Murry. I WILL NEVER FORGIVE YOU FOR WHAT YOUVE DONE.

Siobhan Evans

Weeping quietly, Tara folded the letter again and put it back in the box. There was one more cutting, which she grimly unfolded, determined to see this ritual through. The waves of shame and pain almost had a pleasure to them, in that they took her to her lowest place. She could purge herself through tears.

POLICE USE SCHOOLGIRL 'PSYCHIC' TO TRACK TYLER
A Miston Herald EXCLUSIVE!

Local police failed to find the toddler Tyler Evans because they had been sent on the wrong trail by a so-called 'psychic', according to MP Giles Meadows.

Chief Superintendent Alun Constantine has denied the claim that an unidentified schoolgirl from the Horsley area sent police on a false trail.

Sean Stanley, whose house was the subject of a dawn raid on a tip-off from the 'psychic', has said that this false information prevented police from finding the child early enough to receive vital medical care. A source at Horsley Hospital, where the boy was treated, has confirmed that they may have been able to save his life if he had been found a few hours sooner. The three year old died from injuries sustained on Thursday.

His mother Siobhan Evans and his brother and sister are said to be in deep shock. They are currently being cared for by relatives.

Tara's sobs came from deep inside, wracking her body with spasms of pain and guilt.

She cried hard for some time. Eventually, exhausted and shivering, she pulled the pale green throw that covered her duvet around her arms and stared up at the ceiling with throbbing eyes.

As always, she began to torture herself by remembering how she'd stared up at the entrance to the police station that day. It was like pressing on a painful bruise. She imagined an alternative reality in which she simply turned around and walked away. There was a kind of agonising bliss in picturing this. How she wished she could go back and make it happen.

But she hadn't done that. Instead, she had gone inside and somehow persuaded them to listen to her.

Tara had heard that the three year old had gone missing a few weeks into the spring term. Tyler Evans was the brother of a girl in the year below her, Chelsea. Everyone had been talking about it in class. Tara knew where the family lived; the address was a few streets away from her.

When she'd passed the house on her way home from school, she'd seen a scrum of reporters already forming around the small, neat garden at the front. Outside the garden was one of those yellow bubble cars, the sort every small child in Britain seemed to own. Tara's fingertips brushed across it and then she'd started to go a bit dizzy.

The pictures came, stronger than they had ever been about lost keys or jewellery. So strong they hurt her head and made her feel sick.

A stone angel towered over her, eyes blank and uncaring. Gravestones and statues crowding in. A terrible, hollow feeling of fear only helped by the rough, comforting sensation of a grubby toy pig in her hand.

Tara had staggered away, trying to process what she'd just seen. It was Tyler. She knew this deep in her bones. He was in some sort of . . . graveyard?

She didn't tell anyone. It was too weird. But she spent a whole night tossing and turning as the images bombarded her mind. She told Mum she was sick the next day and as soon as the house was quiet, she'd dressed with shaking hands and walked to the police station.

They hadn't wanted to listen to her at first but then Siobhan Evans was in the station and overheard what was going on. Digging her long nails into Tara's shoulders, she'd made her repeat what she'd just said.

It was Tara's description of the toy that swung opinion towards believing her. No one else knew that Tyler's beloved Piggy was missing too. Siobhan's excitement and insistence that Tara's hunch be investigated made the police act. They had no other information and even though it was obvious the officers Tara met were deeply dubious about this, Siobhan made a scene about the consequences of them ignoring potentially vital information.

So Tara was forced to describe every tiny detail of her images all over again, to several different police officers. Siobhan made Tara hold a baby photo of Tyler on a keyring and more images had come so violently, and in such bright detail, that Tara had retched and almost been sick on the floor of the police station. The images of the statues were so powerful, everyone agreed he must be close to a graveyard. There was a huge cemetery nearby, which served a ten-mile radius. It seemed the obvious place. A massive fingertip search was carried out there, involving police and the many locals who had come out to help.

But there was no sign of Tyler.

Then Siobhan had remembered an old boyfriend who lived next door to a large church in a village about twenty miles away. They'd split under acrimonious circumstances and although Siobhan had no reason to believe the man would take Tyler, there had been threats made during their final, heated row, which implicated him.

The police went in hard, battering down the door and dragging Sean Stanley from where he'd been sleeping off a drinking bender. Already known to police for petty crime, Stanley'd suffered injuries in the police's handling of him.

But Tyler hadn't been there.

As everyone soon discovered, he'd been lying near to his home at the bottom of the steep bank that led to the railway line. An area the police said had already been thoroughly searched. Although obviously not thoroughly enough.

Tara felt about a hundred years old as she wearily began to pack away the cuttings and the letter.

Of course she *hadn't* killed that little boy. His injuries had killed him. And maybe, as her mother had tearfully pointed out many times since, if Siobhan Evans had kept more of an eye on her small son in the first place, it would never have happened.

But it felt like Tara's fault. She couldn't explain what had happened, despite the long tearful hours trying to do just that with Mum and Dad afterwards. She'd been sure, that was all. So sure. And so wrong.

The story would have had more prominence in the national news had it not been for a unique set of circumstances that week: the suicide of a cabinet minister and a massive terrorist attack in France. A perfect storm of bad news.

But it wasn't a big town and it didn't take long for people to find out locally.

There was no need for Siobhan Evans to tell her she'd never be forgiven.

Tara was never going to forgive herself.

Chapter 7

Wind Chimes

The next day at school, Tara was conscious of Melodie Stone's purse in her bag. It felt like it was giving off some kind of radioactive glow. She'd stuffed it hastily into an A4 envelope that morning, and the brief few moments of contact had caused a spasm of pain to shoot through her head. She didn't want to touch it any more than she had to. It was impossible to ignore the thing. Every time she went in her bag to get a book, a tissue or her purse, the bulging envelope seemed to demand her attention.

She found herself next to Karis during food technology, washing up some stuff that Mrs Marchment had used in a demonstration. They worked in silence. Tara kept wrestling with the decision to tell Karis about her conversation with Will. Maybe she could take the flipping purse there instead. But something stopped her every time she formed the words. She didn't want to have to explain how she'd come into contact with Will, in case it meant divulging that she'd been to the lido to find Leo.

So she held back. She wasn't intending to speak at all, but it was Karis who suddenly broke the silence.

'Why did you ask about Mel the other day?' she said.

Tara's breath caught.

'I mean, why wouldn't she be okay in Brighton?' Karis was watching Tara intently, her hazel eyes narrowed.

Tara shrugged. 'You lot were all wailing so much about how sudden it was, that was all,' she said.

Karis sniffed and glanced over to where Jada and co were huddled, giggling over something on Chloe's BlackBerry. Tara followed her gaze. It suddenly struck her that she hadn't seen Karis hanging out with that group for a few days.

'*I* wasn't wailing, actually,' said Karis.

'Whatever,' said Tara, rinsing off a wooden spoon, which was nobbled and sticky with pastry mix, under the hot tap.

'It is a bit strange, though,' said Karis in a rush.

Tara stopped what she was doing to meet her eyes.

'I mean, the fact that her phone isn't working any more,' said Karis. 'Why would she just leave so suddenly? She doesn't even like her dad.'

Tara stared at her. Why did everyone think *she* was the

person to discuss this with?

'Why are you telling me?' she said irritably. 'Can't you share it with your coven over there?' She was surprised at her own daring. Impressed with herself a bit too. She tried to avoid attention and trouble generally. She didn't need any more battles in her life. But Karis didn't turn on her, as she might have expected. Instead she gave a deep sigh. Her hair fell across her face as she wiped in a desultory way at a scuffed plastic chopping board.

'Coven's about right,' she said. They didn't speak for a couple more minutes.

'So how's that gorgeous brother of yours then?' said Karis, flashing a lascivious grin at Tara.

'Trust me,' said Tara, 'you wouldn't think he was gorgeous if you had to use the bath after him. He's so hairy, it's like a gorilla's been grooming itself in there.'

Karis snorted with laughter – a proper, likeable snort – that made Tara grin back at her.

'And,' she added, warming to the theme, 'when he's going out, he checks his reflection in anything remotely shiny. I swear I saw him admiring himself in the kettle before. And the screen of his phone. He checks his hair way more than I do.'

Karis was helpless with laughter now and Tara felt a giggle rumble up from her belly. She wasn't being disloyal to Beck. She just saw a different side to him than other girls, being his sister. Anyway, he could handle it. The laughter felt like internal sunshine.

A dark and then a blond head turned their way from

across the room. She gave Jada the sweetest smile she could muster.

On the way home from school Tara had a feeling of lightness inside. She wasn't exactly friends with Karis, but at least for once she'd had a bit of a laugh with someone here.

It reminded her of her old life, before they moved. Before everything happened, more accurately.

She hadn't ever been one of the popular girls, but she'd done okay. She'd been mates with Mahlia since primary school. They'd gone through everything together; starting secondary school, spots and periods, boys and exams. But she'd moved away too, to Scotland, a few months before things kicked off. Even though they texted and emailed, it was hard to stay friends when you didn't see people, plus Mahlia had changed. She'd gone all active for the first time ever and threw in mentions in her emails and texts of weird stuff like water-skiing on lochs.

Anyway, today had been the best day in a while. It was nice to feel like a normal girl for once.

Tara decided to walk along by the river, which was a slight detour, but more scenic than going by the main road. She walked along, noticing the weeping willow that bowed delicate fronds over the water on the other bank. A wood pigeon cooed gently somewhere above her. The trees were perfectly mirrored in the still water today and she passed a houseboat that sent blue and red splashes onto the murky green of the water. A large woman with grey dreadlocks was watering the plants that tumbled from stone pots on the boat roof. She swayed slightly to the languid thump of reggae music drifting from an ancient speaker on the deck. Seeing Tara, she smiled. Tara gave her a warm smile back.

As Tara walked a little further, houses began to come into view on the opposite bank.

Within a few moments she saw the iron bridge, and groaned. She'd somehow managed to forget about the purse for a little while, but now it looked as though dropping it off would be so easy, it'd be downright mean not to do it.

She put her hand into her bag and fished out the large envelope. It was looking a bit dog-eared after being scrunched up in there all day. In fact, something had leaked in her make-up bag, and there was a sticky pink mark on the top corner. Tara tried to smear it away with the side of her hand.

She looked up again. The houses were three storeys high, and painted white. They looked grand and elegant. Some had carefully landscaped gardens, which led in neat, green steps down to the water, with decking or vast conservatories that gleamed in the sunlight.

One of the houses a bit further along stood out like a broken tooth in a Hollywood smile. Even from this distance Tara could see the blankets pinned up at windows instead of curtains. The back garden was a tangled jungle of brambles and nettles. A giant plastic sunflower on a stick was poking out of the low fence, where it twirled in the breeze. There was an odd tinkling sound coming from that direction and Tara spotted several sets of metal wind chimes hanging from a gnarled old fruit tree in the garden. The house looked shabby and neglected. Tara quickly ruled this out as Melodie's house. Someone like her *definitely* didn't live somewhere like this. She always wore really fashionable stuff and her hair couldn't be cheap to maintain either, Tara thought.

But when she crossed the bridge, she found she wasn't on the road she needed after all. This one curved in the opposite direction to the houses. She had to ask directions in a florist's and the road she was looking for turned out to be several streets over.

Her good mood had totally evaporated now. She was eager to get this pointless exercise over and done with so she could go home. Then she'd text Will. She'd say she didn't want anything further to do with it. Melodie Stone was probably having a lovely time in Brighton with everything money could buy, being a complete bitch to a whole new set of people.

It seemed ages before Tara found herself at the top of a cul-de-sac called Riverdale Rise. She made her way down towards the river to the number Will had written down – ten. It was only when she got to number eight that she realised the house she wanted *was* the shabby one she'd seen from the back.

Well . . . that's a bit of a turn-up, she thought.

There was a small front garden surrounded by tall railings with white paint peeling off them to reveal patches of dark rust. An old bike, missing a saddle, was propped up against the railings. An open bin bag filled with empty wine bottles sagged next to an old dressmaking dummy wearing a greasy-looking baseball hat. The stained grey torso looked eerily like a body half slumped there. Two white lion statues adorned the end pieces of the stone steps. One was missing a head; the other had a bit of bedraggled tinsel tied limply round its neck. Its nose was chipped off, like it had been in a fight.

Tara looked up at the house which, despite all the rubbish garlanded around it, was about four times grander than her own. A pane of glass was broken in the big bay window on the first floor, where a circular dream catcher with faded feathers hung down inside. Paint peeled on the rotten, wooden window frames. Tara glanced at the house on the other side, which had pristine windows showing swagged silky curtains. As she turned her gaze back to number ten, she thought she saw a movement at the window, but it was too fast for her to be sure.

Suddenly determined to get out of there, Tara stepped forward and lifted the heavy door knocker. At that moment though, the door swung open from the inside, making her yelp and stumble back.

'Can I help you, darling?' A tiny, blond woman a bit younger than Mum stood at the door. She had lots of smudgy kohl around sleepy, pale blue eyes and her hair was twisted up into a messy knot on her head. She was wearing a long cream top that was a bit see-through over knee-length off-white leggings. Her small feet were bare, her toenails pale pink. She reminded Tara of a dishevelled fairy.

'Oh, ah, I'm . . .' Tara gabbled and then managed to find her words. 'I'm just dropping this off for Melodie . . . Mel.' She thrust at the envelope at the woman, arm straight out. 'It's her purse. She, ah, she left it at, um, my house.'

The woman hesitated and then took it from her before yawning widely, unselfconsciously showing pink gums like a cat.

'You'll have to excuse me,' she said, 'I was having a little nap.' She had a strange, babyish sort of voice. 'What did you say your name was, darling?'

She hadn't said anything like that of course, but replied, 'It's . . . Tara.'

The woman, presumably the aunt, Faith, that Will had mentioned, scrunched up her brow as she tried to place her. Then she smiled. 'Well, Mel has a lot of friends.'

A loud thud of bass suddenly drowned out her words. A black car pulled into the cul-de-sac and parked at the kerb. The music died suddenly as the engine was turned off. A bald, muscular man in a tight black T-shirt climbed out of the car. He was staring at Tara with an interest that made her skin prickle. He half smiled as he strode up to the doorway, brushing a bit closer than he needed to as he passed.

'Who's this, baby?' he said to Faith.

'This is Tara,' said Faith in a friendly way, 'she's a friend of Mel's. She's brought her purse.'

'Has she now,' he said and his eyes crept up and down Tara's body.

Ugh, what a sleazebag, Tara thought.

As he moved past Faith to get through the front door, he put his hand on Faith's bum and squeezed before leaning over and giving her an open-mouthed kiss, his eyes never leaving Tara's. She could actually see his meaty tongue. This, she guessed, was Ross. No wonder Melodie could be a pain, living with these two horrors. But did Leo live here too?

She shuddered and failed to hide a grimace. 'Thanks, if you can just let her have it, that'd be great,' she mumbled, blushing now.

'Of course, lovely,' said Faith. 'Thanks for dropping by.'

She heard a giggle as the door closed and realised her hands were shaking violently. Wanting to get home more than anything, she happened to glance inside the car as she passed the window. There was a tiny, naked doll hanging from the rear-view mirror.

Creepy.

Tara peered into the car. Something snagged her attention. What was it? She glanced nervously up at the windows of the house but couldn't see anyone looking, so she scooted round to the passenger side and peered in the window.

It was a faded pink scrunchie. Long blond hairs were caught in it.

The edges of her vision darkened and everything seemed to slow down. Tara could hear her own breaths, ragged and laboured, and a feeling of terror clutched at her stomach with an icy grip that made her moan softly. Her chest hurt. It was so dark . . .

No! Stop it. I won't do this again. Tara squeezed her fingernails hard into the soft flesh of her palms and the pain seemed to force her mind back to the reality of where she stood.

A car alarm in the next street shrieked then with ear-splitting aggression and it helped to break the effect. Glancing once more at the tall white house, Tara almost sprinted out of the cul-de-sac and towards the main road.

The idea of walking along the towpath suddenly seemed a lot less attractive than it had earlier. A dull headache began to throb behind Tara's left eye again.

But she'd stopped it, hadn't she? Sort of, anyway. She'd stopped the pictures that were trying to force their way into her mind and, for the first time in ages, it gave her a feeling of control.

When she was a few minutes from her front door, she pulled Will's business card from the pocket in her bag. She looked down at what was written on it.

Will Meadows, Musician.

The words were in arty writing on a plain white backdrop. She reached for her phone and then hesitated. Once Will had her number, he'd probably want her to do something else in his lovesick quest. He'd probably been dumped and just couldn't accept it, she thought, pushing back the images that tried to nudge the back of her mind, telling her Melodie Stone was in danger. Anyway, she'd done what Will asked her to do and now she could just leave the whole thing alone.

She walked over to a litter bin and dropped the card into it before hurrying towards home.

Hunched over the laptop at the kitchen table, Tara's fingers worked at the keyboard with fast clicks. Mum was reading the local paper, tortoiseshell glasses perched on the end of her nose. She made a loud tutting sound and then murmured, 'Gosh, what an awful thing.' But Tara wasn't really listening. She was busy emailing Mahlia for the first time in ages. She'd been meaning to for weeks, and then a sudden craving for the familiarity of her old life finally made her sit down and get on with it.

After a few minutes Mum got up and stretched her arms, yawning widely. 'I'd better get ready for Pilates,' she said, leaving the room.

Tara grunted in response and finished off her email. She sat back in her chair, pleased she'd finally made the effort.

Thirsty now, she got up and walked over to the sink, where she took a glass and filled it with water. She grabbed an apple from the bowl on the counter and walked back to her laptop, already impatient for Mahlia to reply, even though she knew it was far too soon to check.

Crunching into the apple, she glanced at the paper that was still spread across the table. Mum was messy, like

Beck, whereas Tara and Dad liked things tidy and ordered. A picture caught her eye and then the headline above it. Something in her subconscious sent adrenaline coursing through her veins like an injection of iced water.

MUSICIAN CRITICAL
AFTER LATE-NIGHT HIT AND RUN

Tara bent over to look more closely. Dread clutched at her stomach like a cold fist. The picture was of Will, smiling up at the camera as he played a guitar on a picnic blanket. His hair was shorter and his feet bare below his cut-off jeans. His thin ankles looked vulnerable. He looked much younger. Innocent and boyish. She hastily read the piece.

A promising young musician has been left in a coma after being hit by a car late on Wednesday night at the junction of Homerton Road and Eastern Street.

William Meadows, 20, a singer/songwriter who has performed at the Stourton County Festival and a variety of local music venues, was leaving the Mi Casa Bar on Homerton Road at 1 a.m. when a white car or van was seen approaching him.

An eyewitness, Joanna Greenfield of Stamford Crescent said, 'It wasn't going very fast but then seemed to speed up as he went to cross the road. It all happened so fast that I didn't manage to get the number plate or even see what sort of car it was. Only that it was small and white. It may have been a van. All I can say is that I hope the driver will do the decent thing. My prayers are with William and his family right now.'

The musician's mother, Anna Meadows, 55, said, 'Will is the gentlest boy in the world. He's never hurt a soul. All he wants is to make music. How anybody could hurt him and leave him like that is callous beyond belief.'

Doctors at the Princess Royal Infirmary say William is in a critical condition with head injuries. He remains in a coma.

Police say there are no CCTV cameras covering that crossing and they have so far been unable to identify the vehicle. If anyone has any information relating to the crime, please call this number.

Tara's legs suddenly felt wobbly. She sat down at the table, staring at the story until the words stretched and blurred together.

Pictures whizzed through her mind. Will walking along a street, late at night. Maybe a bit drunk. Not concentrating – thinking about Melodie, perhaps – as he steps out into the street. The shock on his face as the car bears down on him, headlights like monstrous eyes. The impact, the pain . . . then darkness. It was almost like she could feel the road rearing up at her like a wall.

She pushed her hair out of her eyes with a shaking hand. This wasn't one of her weird turns. She knew that. It was just her imagination going overboard. But she felt strangely guilty. As though this all had something to do with Melodie and what Will had asked her to do. Maybe he'd been wondering why Tara hadn't texted him, like she'd said she would. Maybe he was so distracted about it that he didn't pay attention as he crossed the road . . .

But she knew that was stupid, really. Any number of things could have been going through his head. And anyway, what had that witness said? That the car seemed to speed up when Will came into sight? That didn't sound as though Will had been to blame. It sounded . . . deliberate.

Tara breathed slowly through her mouth, trying to calm her galloping heartbeat. He'd said Ross had threatened him in some way. Could Ross have done this? But for what reason? Because there really was something to hide about Melodie?

Ross had a black car, but the witness had definitely said it was a white vehicle. Could he have more than one?

Mum came back into the kitchen, humming. Tara had enough time to rearrange her face into an impassive expression and get up to wash her glass as though nothing was wrong. She let her hair fall across her flushed cheeks as she rinsed the glass and put it on the drainer. The last thing she wanted was an inquisition from Mum, who was probably better than the Gestapo at extracting information when she got wind of something. It would be impossible to explain that she vaguely knew Will without Mum wanting to know exactly how she knew a twenty-year-old bloke.

'See you later, sweetheart, okay?' said Mum, grabbing her handbag from the kitchen table and patting Tara's shoulder. 'There's some chicken in the fridge for dinner, bread from that artisan bakery, and salad stuff. Make sure you get some before Beck descends on it like a plague of locusts. You know what he's like when he's had football practice. Or indeed, what he's like on any given day.'

'Yeah, I know,' said Tara, forcing a grin.

'Oh,' said Mum, 'Dad says he's sorry to work late again, but you know how it is with him still being the new boy.'

'Course,' said Tara. 'Have fun at Pilates.'

Her laptop pinged with an email as her mother left the house. She sat down to read it, distractedly. It was from Mahlia, who was so happy to hear from her and so sorry she'd been rubbish about getting in touch and *so* dying to catch up.

Tara's eyes skimmed the email but the chatty words rolled over her without meaning.

She couldn't get the picture out of her head: Will looking up and seeing the car, surprise and then naked terror on his face. The sickening thump as he hit the road.

Could someone have done this to him on purpose? And if so, why?

CHAPTER 8

SKIN

Tara tried to put it out of her mind. She'd caught Karis's eye a couple of times and thought about starting a conversation, but decided against it. Karis was often on the fringes of the Gossip Girls set now. They would be stretched out on the grass, sunning themselves like lizards – lizards with long, tanned legs – and Karis would be sitting slightly to the side, as though she was with them but not with them all at the same time. Tara knew she wouldn't be able to stop herself from asking if Karis had heard about Will's accident . . . or whatever was the right word for what had happened. And she didn't really want to get into that.

Because now she kept thinking about Leo and whether he could have been the person who knocked Will down. Walking home from school, she went over it again in her mind. There was no reason to suspect him in any rational way. He seemed all right, despite his Hard Man look. But Will had mentioned that Leo disapproved of him. And Tara had seen Leo arguing viciously with Melodie the day before she'd gone missing.

Tara made an angry noise in her throat. If anyone had been nearby, they would have thought she was mad, like she was talking to herself. Luckily, no one was.

Missing? Who said anything about Melodie being *missing?* No one had. There was no real reason to think anything had happened to her. As for Will, plenty of hit-and-run accidents happened, especially late at night when people were drunk.

As she got nearer to home, another thought came to her. As far as Leo was concerned, she and Melodie were friends. Was there any harm in getting into a conversation and mentioning she was worried Mel hadn't been in touch? Maybe he could prove to her in some way that the girl was living happily in Brighton and hanging out with celebs. A vivid image of Melodie came into Tara's head then, honey hair swinging down around her neck; eyes creased meanly as she regarded Tara, like Tara was dirt and she was some goddess. It wasn't hard to imagine her living in luxury, not caring that people were worried about her.

Tara didn't care what Melodie Stone was doing. She

only wanted to stop this nagging sensation she couldn't shake off. Plus, she felt bad about Will. She knew where she had to go.

There was a sticky moment later when Mum suggested coming swimming with her, and Tara blurted out that she was meeting a friend from school. Mum couldn't have looked happier. She practically forced a tenner into Tara's hand, saying they could 'hang out together and have coffee after', in a way that made Tara feel a sickly mix of cringing, guilt and love.

The air was hot and still. Tara expected the pool to be busy when she finally got there, feeling a little sticky and uncomfortable in her baggy top that was cut to hang off one shoulder. After debating with herself for a ridiculous amount of time, she'd brought the bikini again, rather than the stout Speedo, just because it went better with the T-shirt. It had nothing to do with Leo, she told herself. She didn't even know what kind of person he was. He might be someone capable of attempted murder.

The girl she'd seen cleaning the pool was at the entry kiosk today. She smiled at Tara, seeming to remember her, as she took the coins from her hand. Tara turned it round to be stamped but the girl waved her own hand airily to signify that there was no need.

Once through the gates, Tara scanned the pool area for Leo. He wasn't there. The old bloke from before – Dobby – was sitting at the side of the pool in a lifeguard T-shirt. Good job she was a strong swimmer, she thought. She didn't much fancy the idea of being rescued by him in a crisis.

Squinting into the sunlight, Tara looked around. The water sparkled like a sheet of diamanté and the sun bounced off the grotty sun loungers, making them seem newer and whiter than they were. There were a few more people than last time: a group of teenagers younger than Tara were messing about in the shallow end, the girls shrieking as one of the boys vigorously churned the water with a skinny arm. The old lady with the daisy swimming cap was there, barely making an impression on the surface of the water. Tara felt an unexpected fondness at seeing her again. In the shallow end an obese woman sat on the side with her toddler, whom she kept dunking like a biscuit into tea while singing a nursery rhyme. The child thrashed its legs and made unhappy noises.

There was one other person, a man, swimming alone in the fast lane, his strong, confident strokes cleanly slicing through the water. As Tara got to the changing rooms she happened to look again and was startled to see that the swimmer was Leo. He was getting out now, the muscles in his strong arms bulging as he pressed down on the pool's edge and levered himself out. His hair was slick and wet. His eyes looked dark and intense as he ran his hand over his face. He was strong but tall and slim too and Tara couldn't help looking at his smooth chest and flat belly. His black swimming shorts clung to the strong curve of his thighs.

'God, get a grip, Tar . . .' she mumbled under her

breath, a hysterical giggle threatening to hiccup out as she hurried into the changing room. *You need that cold water, girl,* she thought. As she got undressed, her hands shook a little. Then it struck her that he was probably at the end of his shift if he was swimming. Disappointment bit harder than it ought to have done.

But when she emerged from the cubicle a few minutes later he was still there.

'Thanks, Dave,' he said. 'I needed that. I'll take over now.'

Dave/Dobby muttered something and, sighing, left the side of the pool. Tara deliberately avoided looking at Leo as she made her way to the steps at the deep end, where she did her usual gradual dip into the water.

She pushed off from the side and swam, her body responding to the water more quickly than it had last time. Then it had been all about remembering long forgotten movements and sensations, but now her limbs seemed to come alive instantly. She did one length, two . . . After ten she stopped counting, losing herself entirely in the rhythm of her strokes. Soon it was as though the water coursed through her, filling her with pure aquamarine light.

Finally, out of breath, Tara swam to the side, her arms and legs shaking now. Her eyes stung and she wished she had remembered to bring her swimming goggles. Thinking about it, she wasn't sure if she still owned any. She'd get some for next time.

Next time? She was surprised by the thought as she climbed the steps out of the water, careful to make sure her bikini bottoms didn't slip down. She tried to subtly rearrange them, glancing upwards and catching Leo's eyes on her. She blushed and started to walk down the side of the pool, when pain screamed through her foot and made her stumble, crying out.

A pink watery stain was already forming around her toes. When she lifted her foot, she saw a jagged bit of glass sticking into the pad of her sole. The pain blazed and throbbed. She stumbled again as she tried to pull it out.

'What happened?' Leo was suddenly there, frowning down at her foot. For a second, hot embarrassment overtook the pain and her face throbbed. 'Did you stand on something?'

'Bit of glass,' she said tightly, angry suddenly at how grotty this pool was. She should have just gone to the leisure centre if she wanted a swim. It would be clean there or, at the very least, not a danger zone.

'Oh look, God, I'm really sorry,' said Leo. 'I *told* Dave to . . . Jeez, look, come on over here. I'll get the first-aid kit.'

His face was concerned even though he avoided looking at her directly. Grudgingly, Tara put her hand on his forearm, which he was holding out to her. His skin was warm, his arm covered in very fine dark hairs. Not like hairy ape Beck, with his coarse fur. This was silky-looking, and she had a mad urge to touch it with her fingertips. Her cheeks flared brighter still as she hop-walked, leaning on him, over to one of the loungers.

'Wait there a sec,' said Leo and he went off to a small room at the side of the pool. Daisy Lady was getting out of the water and she gave Tara a knowing sort of smile.

Cheek! It was like she was suggesting Tara was trying to get Leo's attention when actually her foot was hurting like anything. She glanced down at it, glad, despite herself, that she'd cut her toenails the other night and put on some shimmery blue nail varnish.

Leo came over holding a large white box that looked older than both of them put together.

'I'm really sorry about this,' he said. 'A kid broke a bottle earlier and Dave said he'd cleaned it all up.'

'It's all right,' said Tara. 'Look, I can do this myself . . .'

'It's better if you let me,' he said, still not meeting her eyes. 'I've sort of been trained and we don't want you getting an infection. Is that okay?'

They met eyes then just for a second. Tara slid her gaze away quickly.

'All right,' she said, grudgingly. 'But is it because you're worried I'm going to sue or something?'

Leo smiled as he doused a piece of cotton wool in foul-smelling antiseptic and then used it to carefully clean a pair of tweezers. 'Be my guest. Would serve old Dobby right if you did,' he said. 'Might make him look after the place a bit better.'

'Does he own this place?' said Tara.

Leo gently took hold of her cold, damp foot in his warm, dry hand and, frowning in concentration, tweezed out the piece of glass. Tara gasped as it slid out of her skin and then heard it tinkle into the upturned lid of the first-aid box.

He shot her an apologetic look.

'Worst's over now,' he said. 'Dobby's got some weird arrangement with the council that I don't really understand. I don't bother asking too much. I just take the money and enjoy the free swims.' He looked up at her then, his dark blue eyes intense. 'It didn't go in far, luckily.' He started to clean the cut with yet more antiseptic, and finally put on a large plaster. Funny how he seemed more confident and sure, doing this, than when they'd had casual conversations before.

He worked in silence, which was a relief. Tara was going through such a range of emotions that she felt her voice would come out like Donald Duck's if she tried to speak. The sensation of his warm, gentle hand on her naked foot was almost unbearable. She couldn't work out whether she wanted to kick him away or push him down on the wet poolside and snog his face off. His actions felt too intimate to be happening between strangers but it was also churning up a whole load of feelings she hadn't had since Jay. It felt as though her nerve endings were exposed all over her body, transmitting electricity in a low hum. She could power the National Grid at this rate. Her treacherous cheeks burned and glowed. Shivers tickled up and down the back of her neck and she tried not to imagine Leo's fingers there too.

She tried to tell herself to get a grip. There was no way he was interested in her like that. He was just being kind and doing his job. And who would want a girl who had a face like a tomato? Anyway, she didn't even care.

'All done,' he said, after a few moments.

'Thanks,' she said tightly, when she'd managed to find her voice. 'You've done a good job. It feels much better.'

Leo shrugged. 'Was sort of what I wanted to do for a while.'

He met Tara's puzzled expression.

'You know, paramedic type stuff.'

'Oh,' said Tara. 'You don't any more then?' she said and then felt it was the wrong thing to say. Leo's expression seemed to snap closed.

'Things change,' he said and then rocked back on his feet and stood up. 'Do you want to go and get dry now? You must be getting cold.'

Flustered, Tara got up, suddenly convinced that she'd somehow been taking too much of his time, even though he was the one who'd wanted to sort her foot out.

Then he spoke again.

'Once you're ready, come and find me and I'll sort out getting you home.'

'Oh,' she said, 'it's all right, I can walk.'

She moved away and instantly winced. It *did* hurt a bit. It would take ages to walk home. Maybe she could call Mum or Beck? But she remembered that both were going to be out this afternoon. And for some reason she didn't want them knowing about this place. It would be spoilt if they came here.

Leo was watching her.

'I don't think you should push it. Anyway, it's the least we can do. Go get changed and I'll see you in a minute. Want help walking over there?'

'Er, no, I'm okay,' she said. 'I'll come and find you.'

Hobbling over to the changing room, Tara's mind was racing. This was what she'd wanted, a chance to question Leo. Now she had the perfect opportunity.

But being near him made it hard to think straight. She should just go home and forget about it. *Definitely*, she thought, as she dried herself with the towel and pulled on clothes over her damp, cold skin.

Then she pictured Will lying comatose in a hospital bed. She didn't owe Will anything, she told herself. But if she could just get rid of this nagging feeling that something was wrong with Melodie, and that this something had landed Will in hospital, then she'd be able to move on. Maybe then she could come swimming just for the fun of it, despite the hazards attached.

She spent ages combing her hair through this time. She'd remembered to bring some make-up remover pads to clean under her eyes, and some mascara to replace what had come off in the pool. Plus, she'd stuck some lip gloss into her bag at the last moment. She slicked some on and tried to push her shoulders back, like Mum was always telling her to do, and came out of the cubicle. She saw the girl from the entrance, who gave her a cautious smile.

'I'm really sorry about your foot,' she said. 'Are you all right?'

'Yeah, I'm okay, thanks,' she said.

The girl leant closer with a conspiratorial grin. 'Leo gave Dave hell about it. They had a right old ding-dong. Leo said he was walking if Dave didn't get his arse back over here so Leo could take you home.'

'Oh, dear,' said Tara, feeling even more self-conscious.

The girl grinned and moved away.

Tara couldn't have drawn attention to herself any more successfully if she'd tried. She was half regretting coming here. Only half though, because she kept vividly remembering the feeling of Leo's warm hand on her bare foot. She shivered and made her way back to the entrance.

There was an office in a wooden hut. Leo was in there with his back to her, bending over the computer screen.

She cleared her throat and he turned round with a slight smile.

'How's the foot?' he said, his gaze quickly slipping away from her face.

'It's not too bad,' she mumbled. 'It's probably best if I just get . . .' She pointed in a vague general direction away from the pool but Leo was already picking up car keys.

'Really, it's the least I can do . . .' he insisted.

She was frowning at him and still half looking at the door. He regarded her for a moment and then groaned.

'I'm an idiot. Why would you just get into a car with some bloke you don't know? I'll call for a cab.'

He was reaching into his pocket for his mobile when a flash of determination made Tara speak again.

'It's all right,' she said. 'You're Melo— Mel's brother, aren't you? I'd love a lift, thanks.'

He smiled. 'Okay, if you're sure. I'll just tell Cassie I'm off.'

He disappeared for a moment and then came back, jingling his car keys against his leg. 'Car's this way,' he said and set off at a pace towards the car park. Tara hobbled along behind him until he turned to look at her.

'Sorry, my dad says I only have one setting. Take your time.'

Tara was sure he was going to offer again to help her but then he looked away and walked slowly with her towards the car park.

As Leo approached a car, shock coursed through Tara.

Of course. She should have remembered. She'd seen it before, hadn't she?

Leo's car was white.

CHAPTER 9

BEAUTIFUL

S he quickly swept her gaze over the front of the vehicle. It was rusty and a bit scratched but she couldn't see any bumps or dents. For a second the thought of speeding metal slamming into soft flesh overwhelmed her and she felt dizzy.

'You all right?'

She realised she'd closed her eyes and she coughed, trying to remember what normal looked like so she could attempt to recreate it.

'Fine,' she said. *Come on, you can do this.* She tried to pull open the passenger door, which was resistant to her efforts. Why? Because the car had been in an accident and jammed it closed? Tara's heart began to race.

Leo came round to her side of the car and, with a shy, apologetic grin, yanked the door open.

'It's a bit of a rust-bucket but it'll get you home in one piece.'

Tara shuddered a little inside at his choice of words.

'Where to?' said Leo.

She gave him her address and he gave a short nod of recognition. Inside the car, Tara sat stiffly, trying to make space for her feet in the footwell. It was crammed with a large sports bag and a rolled-up towel that looked as though it had been there for ever. Tara was fizzing with nerves, wondering if she should question Leo, but she had no idea what to say. Plus, she was hyper-conscious of his strong, tanned arm near hers as he clipped in his seatbelt, which obviously was just *wrong* of her, she knew.

He'd just turned the engine on when a panicked, disembodied voice filled car, making Tara jump.

'*They're coming outta the walls! They're coming outta the goddamn walls!*'

As Leo switched off the engine and fumbled in his pocket, Tara realised the sound was the ringtone on his mobile.

He glanced at her, flushing a little. 'It's from *Aliens*,' he said, a bit apologetically, and then answered the call.

'Papi, I'm busy right now. What's . . . ?' he sighed. 'Are you all right? Don't move, I'll be right there.'

He put his phone away and looked at Tara, his expression concerned.

'Look,' he said, 'I have to stop off before I take you home. My dad … he's disabled and he's got himself stuck getting out of the bath. We're on Foley Road so it'll be a quick detour before I take you to yours. Do you mind?'

'No, that's okay,' she said, as the car pulled out of the park. *That's interesting,* she thought, gathering her courage to speak again. 'Don't you live with Mel then?' She was aiming for 'nonchalant' but feared she'd ended up with something closer to 'stiff and weird'.

Leo shook his head. 'No, we've never lived in the same house, thank God. Our family's not exactly your usual two-point-three kids thing,' he said as he expertly pulled onto a roundabout, one forearm resting on the open window in that cocky lad's way.

'Oh?' said Tara, trying not to sound as interested as she really was.

'Our mum, Hope, well, she was what they called a wild child in the Nineties. My pa— my dad's Italian and she met him on holiday in Sicily. He gave up everything to come over here and then she left him when I was a baby.' This had the air of something that had been said so many times that all bitterness had been soaked away by the passage of time. 'Dad stayed here and brought me up,' continued Leo. 'Hope hooked up with Adam Stone and was pregnant with Melodie before I was even walking.'

Tara slid a look at him.

He shrugged. 'That was Hope for you. Or so I'm told.'

'Oh,' said Tara. 'Is she … ?'

'Dead? Yeah,' said Leo. 'It's okay though, because it's

not like I really knew her or anything. She died of a drug overdose when I was three. I don't remember her.'

'And Faith's an aunt, right?' she said with a boldness she wasn't feeling.

Leo slid her an odd look. 'Yeah, she's Hope's sister. She got custody of her because, at the time, Adam was in no fit state to look after a baby. He was in rehab himself.' He grinned. 'I know what you're thinking . . .'

Tara gulped. 'Er, you do?'

'Yeah,' said Leo. 'Faith and Hope. Yes, their parents were hippies.'

Leo glanced at her again. 'But don't you know any of this already?'

'What?'

'Doesn't Mel tell her friends *anything*?'

Tara froze. She'd forgotten about the lie she'd told, that she and Melodie were friends. There may have a been a moment before now when she could have said, 'Actually, when I say friends, I just mean we sit together in English', but now it was too late. Instead, she found herself saying, 'You know what she's like.'

Leo sighed. 'Yeah. Too well.'

No one spoke for another minute or so, and Tara had the sensation of having missed an opportunity that wouldn't present itself again.

They soon turned down a road of terraced houses not far from Tara's school. The houses were small and made from red brick. Many had broken walls at the front. It was a busy main road and traffic thundered by. Leo pulled into a sort of yard behind the houses halfway down the row and stopped the engine, turning to Tara.

'I won't be long,' he said, unclipping his seatbelt. 'Do you want to wait here?'

Tara looked past him to where a group of boys a bit younger than herself were slouched on the wall, or making lazy circles on BMXs. They were, as one, looking at the car.

'Can I come with you?' she said, unclipping her seatbelt.

Leo looked away and there was an awkward pause until he met her eyes again. There was a defiant look in them now, which she couldn't work out.

'Yeah, why not,' he said. 'Come on.'

They trudged across the car park, which led to a row of rusty-doored garages. There were some whistles and catcalls from the boys, which ended abruptly when Leo turned and gave them a look.

He caught her watching and gave her a short smile, which the boys couldn't see. She returned the smile, following him through a rickety gate and into a patch of garden, which was strewn with a couple of old plastic clothes horses and the remains of several motorbikes.

Leo opened the back door. A grubby lace curtain covered the top half of the door, attached to elastic. It was the sort of thing Tara's mum would never allow in her house. Tara felt a little ashamed for thinking of this as she followed Leo into the kitchen.

'Papi? Papi,' said Leo. 'It's me. I have someone with me . . .' he added hastily.

Leo disappeared off down a dark hallway. A rapid exchange in Italian followed between Leo and someone with a deep voice who must be the mysterious 'Papi'.

It seemed to go on for ages and was so fast that Tara didn't recognise a single word, despite the short-lived fad Mum'd had for learning the language once, and insisting on trying it out on her family.

Unsure what to do, Tara lingered by the back door, looking around an ancient kitchen. The cooker was an electric ring one and there was a washing machine that looked about two centuries old. None of the appliances were built in, like in Tara's kitchen, but free standing and a bit wobbly looking. A yellow formica table was in the middle of the room. An avalanche of papers looked set to slide any minute onto a floor made from large brown carpet tiles, which were a little tacky underneath Tara's sandals.

Her foot began to throb then. She was suddenly hungry and tired. She thought about Mum saying there was bread from the artisan bakery and felt a little throb of shame at how different her own home was from this one, coupled with a strong wish to be there right now.

Leo came back into the kitchen, looking annoyed. Behind him, a dark-haired man using one of those old-people walkers was shuffling along. In fact, he was probably only about Dad's age. He had glasses and a big toothy smile.

There was another rapid-fire burst of Italian. Tara caught the words 'Leonardo' and 'bella'. Tara knew this meant 'beautiful' or 'pretty girl' and instantly blushed hard.

'Dad, this is Tara; Tara, my dad Gianni.' Leo's face was stiff; his voice flat. He looked as though he couldn't wait to get out of there. Tara hoped he had explained why she was there and kept shooting desperate glances at him.

Gianni held out his hand, still beaming. Tara took it and they shook.

'Is pleasure to meet you, Tara,' he said. His rich, warm accent made her imagine sunshine sparkling on blue water.

'You too,' she said with a shy smile.

'Right, you got everything you need then?' said Leo briskly. 'Because I need to shoot off and take Tara home, then get back to the pool.'

'Why you working at a pool when you should be in college, I never know,' said Gianni with a gloomy expression.

'Not now, Papi.' Leo's tone could have cut paper.

Gianni's raised his hand, palm up, in surrender. 'Okay, okay, I shut my mouth. Look.' He mimed zipping his lips, his bright eyes merry.

Tara smiled back, infected by his warmth.

'Come on, Tara,' said Leo with a sigh, 'let's get you home.'

They got back into the car in silence and Leo started the engine. He wasn't talkative now. In fact, he was glowering as they came out of the yard and moved into the stream of traffic.

Tara felt compelled to fill the space. She wanted to know what was wrong with Gianni but didn't dare ask. But then Leo spoke.

'Dad was a roofer,' he said with no introduction. 'Well, actually,' he corrected himself, 'he was an acrobat back in Palermo when Hope met him.' He glanced at her and smiled ruefully. 'No word of a lie. He really was. Never had a single accident. Then he came to this country and the only work he could get was as a roofer. He came off a roof a few years back and broke his back. He can walk a bit now but . . . things are really hard for him. He gets chest infections quite a lot because his upper spine was damaged.' He gave a heavy sigh. 'In fact, we were at A and E all Wednesday night.'

Leo stopped speaking abruptly, biting his own sentence off. His cheeks were flushed and Tara understood somehow that he felt he'd been too open with a stranger. Should she ask about Will? Swallowing, she spoke before she could talk herself out of it.

'What d'you think of Will then?' she said and hardly dared breathe, as Leo flicked a look at her. But his face was completely impassive and gave nothing away.

'I think he's a poser and a moron,' said Leo. 'Why?'

Tara had to suppress a shocked laugh inside, despite the circumstances. Then she remembered why she was asking and felt a spasm of guilt.

'He's had an accident,' she said, forcing herself to go on. 'A bad one.'

'God, really?' said Leo, looking sharply at her. 'What happened?'

'Car hit him,' she said, still hardly daring to breathe. 'He's in a coma.'

Leo gave a low whistle. 'Poor bloke. I don't like him much, but that's bad. Wonder if Mel knows yet.'

Tara thought quickly. Leo seemed genuine, but she didn't really know him at all. The gruff-but-kind-of-gentle exterior might be a complete front. She thought of an expression of her dad's then. *In for a penny, in for a pound* . . .

She took a deep breath and then let the words come. 'Look, can I ask you something?'

Leo turned and glanced at her, with a frown. 'Yeah . . .'

She had to get this right. She couldn't let on that she wasn't really a friend of Melodie's. Not now. It was too late. Hopefully he would never have to know.

'I know this is really stupid,' she said in a rush, 'but me and some of Mel's mates are a bit worried because she's not answering any messages since she went away.'

Leo's expression revealed nothing at these words. He concentrated as he turned right onto another main road. They weren't far from where Tara lived now.

'Well, you know what she's like with stuff like that,' said Leo.

Tara wanted to scream at him. *No, I don't! Other than being a bit up herself and nasty, I have no idea what the hell Melodie bloody Stone is like!*

Tara forced a strangled laugh of agreement but pressed

on. 'Thing is, though, some of them have started saying that something's . . . happened to her.'

Leo turned and looked at Tara properly now. She still couldn't read his expression and then he hooted a short laugh. 'Nothing like a bit of melodrama, is there?' said Leo. 'Let me guess. Jada reckons she's been kidnapped?'

Tara laughed too, a laugh that was clear and false. She wondered if he could hear her echoing heartbeat reverberating around the car.

'Yeah, typical Jada.' Tara tried to soften her tone. 'Uh, bless her.'

What was she talking about?

But he didn't seem to notice her oddness.

'You can tell Jada she's fine,' he said, 'or at least, she was two days ago. Not sure how she'll react to hearing about Will though.' The car turned into Tara's road and she directed him towards her house. As they pulled up at the kerb, Tara was about to say thanks and goodbye, trying to ignore the sensation of something gluing her to her seat, when Leo spoke again.

'Listen to this.' He reached into his trouser pocket and got out his mobile. He tapped the screen and then a familiar, disembodied voice rang out. Chills crept up the back of Tara's neck and she clenched her fists so her nails bit into her palms. But the voice didn't bring on any strange images. *Thank God,* she thought, listening to the words filling the car.

'Babes, know you're having a swim at this time but wanted to say I'm safe and sound. And, ya know . . . sorry about all that the other day. Adam's taking me out for oysters later. You can think of me when you're having fish fingers with Gianni. Speak soon, love you, byeeee!'

There was some kind of noise in the background of the call that was slightly familiar, but Tara couldn't place it. She tried to remember visits to Brighton long ago and what it might have been. But it was quickly gone and unimportant anyway. Melodie was clearly all right. She knew she should be relieved. She should be, but she still felt uneasy.

Leo grinned at Tara. 'Think that will reassure the overactive imaginations?'

Tara grinned back. 'Yeah, I'll pass it on.'

She thought about Will again. Melodie probably hadn't had the guts to tell him he was dumped. Poor Will. Tara wondered if he had regained consciousness yet. She still wanted to know what Leo and Melodie had been having such a heated argument about when she'd seen them in the underpass but couldn't think how she could ask.

'You close then?' It was the best she could do.

Leo made a face. 'We have our moments. Fight like cat and dog sometimes. Well, often, I guess. But we look out for each other too. You got any? Sisters, I mean?'

'A brother,' said Tara. 'But we're the same. Cat and dog.'

There was a pause.

'Okay,' she said, 'thanks for the lift.'

'No problem,' said Leo. 'Least I can do. Hang on a

minute . . .' He undid his seat belt and stretched over into the back seat to reach for something. His T-shirt rode up to reveal the soft angle of his hip bone, smooth but also sharp under tanned skin. Tara's insides flip-flopped unhelpfully. She looked away.

Leo had a roll of tickets in his hand. He pulled off a few and handed them to Tara with his eyes aimed slightly to the left of her head.

'Compensation,' he said. 'That is . . .' he paused, '. . . if you haven't been put off for life.'

Tara took the tickets with a smile, but she wasn't looking at Leo either. It would have felt too intense and she wasn't sure she could take it right now. Her head might actually explode and that would be quite embarrassing, not to mention messy.

'I'll risk it,' she said, gathering up her swimming bag and shoving the car door. It opened quite easily from the inside. 'Thanks. Expect I'll see you then.'

'Yeah, see you.'

Tara heard the car sputtering away back up the road as she turned her key in the door. Her mouth was curled into a smile that felt wholly out of her control.

No one was home and she glided through the house depositing her wet things in the wash basket and hanging up her towel. She felt floaty inside, like a helium balloon that could rise up over the rooftops and on towards the mountains.

Leo was nice. Really nice. Not at all how she'd expected him to be. Selfish Melodie was just moving on from her old life, wasn't she? Tara had the proof now.

But then she thought about the fight she'd witnessed by the river. And Will lying in a coma in hospital. She stopped in the middle of the landing and chewed on her thumbnail.

Really, she didn't know Leo at all.

CHAPTER 10

SALT

That evening, she found herself endlessly replaying the conversation with Leo over in her head and forensically analysing it for meaning.

He really didn't seem like someone who would cold-bloodedly knock someone over. And what reason would he have to do it anyway? Just because he didn't like Will? If Tara knocked down everyone she didn't like, it would be a full-time job.

Anyway, what did it matter? Leo wasn't interested in her. He felt bad about her foot, that was all. He'd prefer girls with poise and oozing confidence, not tomato-headed freaks like her. And hadn't she promised herself to stay away from boys for a while? Or even, for ever?

The way Jay had made her feel still felt like an open wound.

Was it ever going to scab over?

She'd taken a while to go out with him, knowing his reputation as a player – someone who used girls up and threw them away when he was finished with them. When he'd first started to notice her, she'd enjoyed the heat of his gaze as she walked by, but didn't think anything of it. So she had ignored him for a while and worked on her withering put-downs, which he seemed to find incredibly funny. She'd felt it was like when she rubbed Sammie's head really hard with her knuckles: it was surely just this side of painful, but seemed to provoke a glassy-eyed sort of gratification too. Rough love, you might say.

After a while Jay began to fall into step with her. He made her laugh. He was genius at voices and could mimic everyone from his own mates to people off the telly. Her defences quickly started to crumble after those stolen kisses at the pool party, when he'd whispered that he could feel himself falling for her. She'd realised she felt the same and a couple of perfect weeks followed, which even now in her memory seemed bathed in a sort of Hollywood golden light. Then he'd started to push her, wanting more than she was prepared to give. One night, at a Sixth Former's Christmas party, she'd ended up locked in a cupboard with him. He'd been drinking vodka and kissed her too roughly, too insistently. It had shocked her, his unwillingness to listen. They fought. She went home, and that night she debated whether she wanted to stay with someone like that. She wasn't the sort of girl who behaved like a boy's possession. If Mum had taught her anything, it was self-respect.

But when she went into school, she discovered Jay had been spreading ugly rumours about her, which seemed to float like smoke around the school for weeks. She never spoke to him again. When the whole Tyler thing exploded and people at school found out she was the 'schoolgirl psychic', she'd caught him whirling a finger to the side of his head and rolling his eyes to signify madness, prompting hysterical laughter from half the school.

She'd loved Jay and he'd humiliated and hurt her. She couldn't let that happen again.

At dinner, Tara was distracted and not very hungry. She pushed her spaghetti around her plate in circles with her fork. Could Leo have run Will over? But why would he? And he seemed so kind, the way he'd tended her foot, the obvious care he took in looking after his dad . . .

A realisation came to her so suddenly she let out a barely audible gasp.

Hadn't Leo told her his dad had taken ill on Wednesday night? That they had been at A and E all night?

It wasn't exactly proof of his innocence. But it was good enough for Tara.

'What are you grinning about?'

Dad's voice brought Tara back to the present. Her head shot up. All three of her family members were staring at her.

'Hey, are you with us, sweetie?' said Dad.

'Yeah, course,' said Tara, dipping her head again. She piled spaghetti on a fork, and half-heartedly swirled it into her mouth.

'Did you hear what Mum was saying then?'

'No, what was it?'

Mum rolled her eyes but was smiling. 'Me and Dad are going away for my birthday. Is that okay with you? Dad's treating me to a mini-break at a hotel in the Yorkshire Dales.' She peered anxiously at Tara, who hadn't responded yet. In truth, her mind was still on Leo.

'Will you be all right here, just you and Beck?'

'Yeah, fine,' said Tara, distractedly. 'You have fun.'

They still stared.

'*What?*' she said in frustration. 'I said okay!'

She knew she should stay away for a couple of days. The willpower this required was so immense, it almost hurt.

But as it turned out, she didn't need to go to the pool to see Leo again.

She'd been walking Sammie after school and was almost home when she saw his car parked across the road. Her heart skipped as Leo climbed out. His expression was hard to read because he was wearing his sunglasses, but as he got closer she saw his mouth was curled into a hesitant smile. He had on a light blue T-shirt today, which made his skin seem more toasty in colour, along with narrow jeans and black Vans. Tara didn't really notice what boys wore as a rule, but every time she saw Leo her eyes were greedy for details – from the way his watch-face was slightly twisted on his slim wrist, to the tiny scar that bisected his right eyebrow.

Her palms were sweaty and she scrunched her hands into fists. The usual heat was spreading, uncontrolled, and flooding her face. Every part of her was prickling and uncomfortable. She wondered for a second if it was possible to actually die from embarrassment. Maybe she would be the first.

But why was he here? What did he want?

'All right?' said Leo. He took off his sunglasses and she saw his eyes flick nervously towards Sammie, who bounded up and began bombarding him with his brand of doggie love, tail swishing and nose nudging at Leo.

'Sammie, come here,' said Tara sharply. The dog ignored her and began to lick Leo's trouser leg. 'Sammie!' She grabbed the dog's collar and clipped on his lead again. 'Sorry,' she said, blushing even more. 'He's just saying hello, that's all.'

'Right,' said Leo, swallowing visibly. 'I'm more of a cat person, I guess.'

Tara smiled. Her heart was thumping in her ribcage. Her cheeks seemed to get even hotter. Why was he here? As though guessing her question, Leo held out his hand, which contained a girl's purse.

Tara's purse.

'This yours?' he said. 'I found it in the changing rooms.'

Tara let out a gasp of surprise. She hadn't even noticed its absence. The feeling of embarrassment grew more acute then. What did she think he was here for? He was only doing an errand. Nothing else. And the irony wasn't lost on her that she knew where other people had lost things, but hadn't even noticed her own belongings were missing. It was all completely skewed.

'Oh,' she said. She couldn't bring herself to smile again. Her cheeks felt stiff. It felt like she'd flung her arms around his neck or something and been rejected, even though that was silly. 'Thanks.'

Leo cleared his throat.

'Also,' he said, 'I was wondering whether you fancied a free swim later.'

Tara gave him a puzzled smile. 'I have tickets, remember?'

'Ah, but the pool closed early today,' said Leo with a shy, appealing smile. 'Dobby's had to go off somewhere. You could have the pool completely to yourself.' He paused and then cleared his throat, avoiding her eyes for a moment. 'Well, apart from me being there too.'

Tara hesitated. 'Oh, I don't know . . .'

Leo took a step back, and shoved his hands into his pockets. 'Ah, look, I'm not being a perve. It seemed like a nice idea earlier, but I hadn't thought it through properly.' His eyes flicked to Sammie again, as though he expected the dog to defend his mistress's honour and go for him.

But the dog had slumped to the path, tired by his walk, tongue lolling like a long pink slice of ham, and heavy breaths shaking his body.

Incredibly, Leo was actually blushing now. This gave Tara a flash of courage.

'Are you sure it would be okay?'

He looked up again, his eyes hopeful now. 'Yeah, definitely. I have the keys.' He patted the pocket of his jeans and smiled.

Heart drumming, Tara tried to push her hair casually back from her face, where it was flopping down. But her hand was shaking and her face glowed. She was bad at casual when it came to Leo.

'Okay,' she said, 'I would like a swim. I can come over at about, what, five?'

Leo nodded. 'Great, I'll be there.'

He headed off back to his car.

Tara turned away towards her house, and suddenly wanted to skip like she was six years old again.

Getting away proved to be harder than she anticipated. Mum was determined to 'catch up', it turned out. She was really going for it with the meal when Tara was hoping to have only a sandwich until after swimming. Instead, there was going to be lasagne and salad and even homemade garlic bread. She'd put a little bowl of flowers on the table too and even put proper side plates out, like they were in a restaurant. Tara groaned internally.

Mum was vigorously whipping cream in a bowl to go

with strawberries. Tara idled nearby, trying to work out what to say. She quickly decided that a lie was the only possible solution.

'Is it all right if I have mine later?' she said tentatively, picking up a strawberry from the bowl and biting into it. Sweet juice ran over her lip and she stifled a sigh of pleasure at the intense taste. It was the strawberriest strawberry ever. Even the glass of tap water she'd drunk just now was colder and sweeter and *better* than water usually was.

It was as though someone had come along with a big set of paints and made the world more colourful too; even the light was sharper and more crisp. Maybe it was just because it had rained earlier. Or maybe it was the thought of the swim later, just her and Leo in the water . . .

Mum was staring at her. Tara's attention jerked back to the present. She smiled weakly.

'One, stop pinching the dessert,' said Mum, tapping Tara's hand lightly with a finger, 'and two, I wanted us all to be together tonight. Why? Where are you wanting to be?'

Don't blush, Tara willed herself. *Just DON'T BLUSH.* She blushed.

Tara pulled her hair across her face as though she was playing with it, in an attempt to hide the flush staining her cheeks.

'Some mates at school have invited me round to go swimming with them at the pool.' It *was* a pool, so that bit was true. It just wasn't the pool her mum would think she meant, with or without the mythical BFFs.

She could see Mum's mixed emotions playing across her face. She plastered on a pleading smile to her own, jutting her bottom lip and putting her palms together, prayer-style.

Mum let out a big sigh but Tara could see she was pleased by the warmth in her eyes.

'I don't know . . .' She beamed then. 'Between you and Beck, you wear me out with your social lives.'

Tara grinned back, relieved, even if she felt a nudge of sadness at Mum's optimistic words. She'd known the 'friend' thing was her trump card. She knew how much her parents worried. Even if no one ever spoke about it, directly, the events in February still invaded their space.

Later, she stood outside the lido, trying to calm her cantering heart rate. She'd had to carefully time her journey so she wouldn't be early. This had meant having to do a lap round the block to kill some time. And that had made her too hot. Now, she wiped her damp palms along the sides of her favourite green tunic dress and then looked down to check it wasn't magically longer, shorter, bigger or smaller than when she'd left the house. She gave it a tug anyway and stepped forward, trying to lift her chin confidently.

It struck her then that she didn't know how she would get in. There was a metal meshed door across the entrance so she could see into the pool. She knocked tentatively against the rough metal wire and it rattled noisily.

Leo appeared on the other side. His eyes met hers only for a second. Could it be that he was nervous too? He came forward and opened the door with a heavy bunch of keys. Tara had a momentary desire to flee but then he looked up and smiled. Something loosened in her chest and belly. He was wearing long swimming shorts, a short-sleeved checked shirt and flip-flops.

'Hey,' he said quietly. 'You came then.'

'Looks like it.' She followed him into the pool area. It seemed tidier than usual. The loungers had evidently been given a bit of a wipe down. The cool turquoise water of the pool lay like a silk sheet, free of floating leaves and crisp packets.

'Like what you've done with the place,' she said and Leo gave a short laugh.

Goose pimples rose on Tara's arms. The thought of getting undressed and stepping into cold water seemed ridiculous.

'You can have the pool to yourself if you want,' said Leo, his voice almost a whisper again. 'I can go in after.'

'It's okay,' said Tara hurriedly. 'You can swim if you like. I don't need the whole thing to myself.'

Leo's face relaxed a little. 'Right,' he said, 'see you in there.'

He was regretting inviting her here, she could tell. Maybe she shouldn't have come . . .

Leaving now would be downright weird, she reasoned, so she headed off to a changing room. She glanced back to see Leo peel off his shirt and kick off his flip-flops before he dived neatly into the deep end. So easy for boys.

She spent a while getting comfortable in her bikini, fussing about whether it covered everything it needed to cover. And the opposite. She finally emerged from the cubicle, wondering if she was giving Leo the wrong impression by coming here.

Her shoulders were hunched over, her arm across her belly protectively, when she stepped out onto the poolside. She'd never felt so pale-skinned in her life and she had a savage longing for tanned limbs like never before. Surely she was glowing with her bluey-whiteness, like the neon planets she'd had on her bedroom ceiling when she was little.

But Leo wasn't looking at her. He was swimming with long, efficient strokes, his dark head emerging and dipping, seal-like, eyes hidden under his swimming goggles, the water fanning like angel wings behind him.

Tara plunged down the steps and entered the water far quicker than her usual hesitant dipping. She badly needed to do something, anything, with her awkward body. She pushed away from the edge and swam, determined to ignore Leo going the other way.

This was better. Soon she began to relax, concentrating only on the sensation of cutting through the cold, silky water.

She swam length after length until her arms and legs began to tingle with fatigue. Best not to dive today. Her hair probably looked bad enough anyway. She had a sudden, vivid image of herself wearing a hat like Daisy

Lady. What would Leo think about that? She suppressed a surge of giggling inside.

When she climbed out, Leo was standing by the sun loungers, dressed again and in dry shorts. The checked shirt stuck damply to his chest. Tara forced her eyes to swerve from the perfect golden triangle at the V of the collar.

She flashed a damp smile at him and headed for the changing room, unclear about what was going to happen next. Her skin tingled with anticipation and nerves.

She got dressed and tied the belt on her green tunic dress with trembling hands, trying to arrange the slashed neckline at the most flattering angle. She combed through her hair and twisted it into a messy bun, pulling some strands down so it wouldn't look too neat. She squinted into the small round mirror she kept in her swimming bag. Her hair looked too artful and deliberate now. Tara hastily pulled it down again and ruffled it a bit around her shoulders. That would have to do.

The sky was overcast when she emerged from the changing room but the air was soft and warm on her bare arms. In the distance she could hear laughter and voices from what sounded like an evening football match. Floodlights from the pitch bathed the lido in a yellow glow. A car alarm in the distance blared and then stopped. The pool water lapped gently at the tiles around the edge, a gentle breeze ruffling the surface. The details of everything seemed pin sharp but this wasn't the scary pixelated sensation she had during her funny turns. It was like being even more alive than usual. It was the opposite of those bad feelings, in fact. They took her somewhere dark; here everything was light.

Leo had put a picnic blanket on the grass. Technically, it was a faded sheet as far as she could tell, but it was still a nice touch.

A bulging carrier bag sat on the sheet. Tara looked at Leo questioningly. He made a vague gesture at the bag, avoiding her eyes.

'My dad,' he said, 'he cooks, like, all the time. There was a load of stuff we're never going to eat and I thought I'd bring it, you know, in case you were hungry after the swimming. But it's all right, you don't have t—'

'Brilliant,' said Tara at the same time, 'I'm starving.'

They both laughed. Leo dropped down onto the sheet to open the containers. Tara came over and sat, delicately pulling her dress down as it rode up. Sitting on the ground hadn't been in the plan when she'd chosen her outfit earlier.

She gazed down at the various Tupperware containers. There was fancy bread, olives, some sort of cakes that looked a bit like cream horns, and slices of salami.

'Ooh, this looks great,' she said and bit into a piece of bread, which was salty and oily and about the best thing she'd ever tasted. A wash of shame came over her for her snobby thoughts in Leo's kitchen before.

'It's focaccia,' said Leo. 'Homemade. You've got to have one of these as well.' He nudged the container with the cream horn things towards her. 'They're called cannoli.

They're like heart attacks on a plate, but they're kind of great too.'

It seemed a strange thing for a boy to say. Tara finished the bread and bit into a cannoli. Creamy sweetness exploded in her mouth and soft flakes of pastry rained down onto her dress. It took some effort not to groan. Only then did she notice Leo wasn't eating much but picking at the olives.

'See what you mean,' she said, as she finished it. 'Lovely, though. He's a brilliant cook, your dad.'

'Yeah,' said Leo ruefully, 'bit too good.' He caught her puzzled look. 'I was a real porker when I was a kid.' He made a funny face, puffing out his cheeks.

'Really?' she said.

He nodded.

Tara was surprised. She couldn't imagine Leo had ever been anything but gorgeous. Maybe that was why he wasn't as confident as he might be, given the overall package. Maybe that was why he seemed a little shy.

'Yep.' He leant back and rested his head on his hands, looking up at the sky, which was pearly grey now. 'Got bullied all the time. So I got to Year Nine and I decided to do something. Started swimming.'

Tara didn't know what to say, but somehow it seemed okay to say nothing at all.

Leo bought Diet Cokes from the machine and he took a long drink from his can. Tara watched his Adam's apple bob gently in his tanned throat out of the corner of her eye. Then she picked at a thread on the sheet, eyes down.

It took a few moments to realise it was raining. It was only when dark splotches began to star the sheet that they jumped to their feet. She helped Leo hastily gather up their stuff as the sky seemed to rip open and rain pounded on their heads and shoulders. Laughing, Leo grabbed the sheet and remaining food, Tara the towels and wet swim stuff.

Leo gestured to the loungers that were protected by a jutting section of roof. He sat down on one. Tara sat down uncertainly on the next one along. They were facing each other, their knees almost touching. His, strong and brown as toast, hers, pale as snow.

The sky was blue-black now, bruised and boiling. The pool was studded by plopping raindrops. It was dramatic and beautiful. It felt like anything could happen here. Anything at all.

'Do you deliberately make it rain every time I come to this pool?' she said and then shivered as she realised Leo was looking at her intensely, not smiling.

She smiled anyway, self-consciously pushing back the hair that fell across her face. Time seemed to stop. She felt aware of every single centimetre of him, as though heat throbbed from his skin, but maybe it was her who was burning up.

Leo leant over and gently touched her lips with his. Shivers ran down her arms and back, and she opened her mouth a little bit and kissed him back. He tasted of salt from the olives. His warm hand cupped the side of her face.

The rain pounded in a steady beat, splashing hard on

the tiled floor. Tara's feet were getting wet, her toes slippery in her sandals. The kiss went on, deeper and more intense, and then Tara pulled away. She'd had a sudden memory of kissing Jay, flustering her. Look how *that* turned out. She remembered how much it had hurt. Wasn't she supposed to be protecting herself from this happening again?

Neither of them spoke.

'I'm glad we're not having an awkward silence, anyway,' said Leo after a few moments.

A laugh burst from Tara and she looked at him, grateful he'd eased the intensity of the atmosphere.

'Was that . . . okay?' he said, his eyes navy blue in the fading light. 'I mean, was it okay that I did it?'

'It was definitely okay,' said Tara, her voice a bit husky. She had to cough and clear her throat. 'There was someone where I lived before and he . . .' She swallowed. The last thing Leo would want was her getting all heavy on him. Didn't boys hate that stuff? But he did seem different to a lot of boys . . . Different enough to give Tara the courage to be honest. 'Well, he hurt me. You know. A lot. He was a real piece of work.' She looked up, emboldened. 'But that was more than okay.'

Leo was looking into her eyes intently. She could see flecks of gold in the dark blue of his irises. The tiny scar through his eyebrow seemed whiter, more sharply drawn than she'd ever noticed before.

He smiled and then leant over, kissing her very gently again.

The rain thrummed and pounded around them. It was

like being in a bubble; protected from the world.

Some time later, as Tara began to feel quite lost, Leo pulled away and checked his watch. He groaned, then leapt up in one fluid motion. 'Park closes soon so we'd better get going. I'll drive you home.'

He smiled down at her. Tara smiled back, glowing inside.

The windscreen wipers throbbed and swished in a soothing rhythm, which added to the pleasant heaviness in Tara's limbs. She'd like to have driven around all evening, listening to the rain and smelling Leo's warm, chlorinated skin so close. He caught her eye and grinned, prompting warmth to ooze through her again. The headlights of cars were caught by the puddles in the road so they flashed gold.

As they approached Tara's road, she asked him to pull in down the street a little way, to prevent the third degree from Mum when she got in. He turned off the engine and looked at her. She felt shy now, unsure what to do, but Leo leant across and kissed her quickly, a gentle pressure on her lips. He smiled.

'I'm glad you came tonight,' he said.

'Thanks for the swim,' she whispered. 'And the picnic. Tell your dad I liked his food.'

Leo grinned. 'Better not. You'll never hear the end of it. Here . . .' He reached for his phone. 'Let's swap numbers.'

They did so, exchanging shy, pleased grins too. Tara

noticed another missed call from an unknown number. Must have been when she was swimming.

'See you at the pool?' Leo said.

She grinned. 'Oh, I expect so.'

'When?' he said.

'Soon. Not sure when.' She knew better than to be too keen. 'Night.' She leant over and gave him a quick peck before opening the door and almost tumbling out onto her wobbly limbs.

Tara tried to replay the entire evening in her head, but it infuriated her that she had already forgotten tiny details. What was Leo's exact expression when he'd moved in for the first kiss? How long had it really gone on for? She wished she could watch it all, like a film, pressing pause on the kiss so she could live through it all over again.

So much for protecting her heart, she thought. It already felt too late for that. Maybe she deserved a chance at happiness after all?

Chapter 11

Knife

Tara glided around for most of the evening with a dreamy expression on her face. No one noticed, thankfully. Before bedtime, she was looking for her lip balm and remembered it might be in her messenger bag. She padded downstairs in her slipper socks to find it. Mum and Dad were watching television, and didn't hear her coming down. She was grateful, hoping to keep the delicate bubble of time with Leo around her a little longer. She didn't want to talk to anyone else.

She found her bag and took it back up to her bedroom. Then she dumped the contents out onto the bed. Distractedly, she rifled through the books that lay scattered over the green throw.

She quickly found the lip balm under her history book but as she went to remove the lid, her hands stopped and her breath froze in her throat.

The silver treble clef earring she'd found in Melodie's locker lay there, accusingly.

Tara's stomach clenched. She'd forgotten she'd dropped it into her bag. Should she give it to Leo? But how would she explain having it in the first place? She should have thrown it away when she had the chance. Tara reached for the earring and as her fingers made contact, the walls seemed to suck inwards. Her heart pounded in a slow, sickening rhythm that hurt her chest and her throat seemed to close. The familiar bedroom around her faded and again she saw the single lightbulb swinging over a narrow cot bed, where she could now see a figure lay hunched.

Tara gasped and tried to pull herself away but it was too late. Images flashed inside her head with sickening speed, coming and going as though lit by a strobe light.

A figure hunched over, holding a knife. Water lapping somewhere nearby with rhythmic slaps.

The delicate skin of an inner arm. The knife drawing ever closer . . .

Shhh . . . it'll only hurt a little bit . . . be brave.

The blade cutting into soft flesh. White-hot agony.

No! Stop!

Words typed onto a piece of paper.

YOU HAVE TILL FRIDAY
THEN WE'LL CUT HER SOME MORE.

Please . . . I'm frightened! Help me! Someone!

With a sharp cry, Tara threw the earring out of her bedroom window.

Nauseous and icy cold, she pulled her legs to her chest and rocked, head resting on her knees.

'Oh God, why me?' she whispered. 'Why does this keep happening to me?'

She started to cry softly and lay back against the cushions on her bed, staring up at the ceiling even though her eyes burned and throbbed. She was too frightened to close them. Who knew what she might see?

After a while she fell asleep. She dreamt she was wrapped in chains at the bottom of the lido pool. Someone was smiling down at her and she knew she was going to die soon. Then the face became a stone angel. It had Melodie's cold, pretty features and it gradually began to topple towards her.

She woke up and found she was crying again.

Why wouldn't it all just stop? She shook her head, trying to clear away the memories of what had happened earlier. The knife. The threat about something happening. On Friday? This Friday?

'STOP IT!' Her voice sounded shockingly loud in the slumbering house.

Her mouth was bone dry and she took a long drink from the water bottle at the side of her bed. The pale glow of her alarm clock showed four a.m. The house was quiet, apart from the sounds of ticking pipes and the comforting rumble of Sammie's snores from outside in the hallway. She got out of bed and tiptoed out the door. The dog woke up instantly and sleepily thumped his tail against the base of his basket in greeting. She tapped her thighs and he groaned to his feet, ambling towards her, ever hopeful of an impromptu meal or walk. The dog wasn't allowed in any of the bedrooms, but Tara's was the only one on the ground floor. No one needed to find out. She doubted she was going to sleep now and she'd push him back to his own bed before anyone else got up.

She couldn't be alone tonight. Even the smelly old dog was better company than none.

A few minutes later, Tara lay wrapped in a blanket on her bedroom floor. She'd placed her bedroom lamp on the other side of the bed so it cast a gentle glow. The room was wreathed in shadows. The dog's heavy warmth next to her was a comfort and she stroked his velvety head until he gave a blissed-out sigh and then resumed his gentle snores.

It was the first time she'd dreamt about the statues in this house. For a time, this had happened every night. And not just dreaming of them. Seeing them in her mind's eye like flash-carding photographs. The cold, expressionless eyes raised up. Headstones with stark dates carved into the marble. And the deep cold feeling in her bones that spoke of dead things.

She should have been drifting to sleep and remembering Leo's lips on hers. Instead, she was fighting off images of death and pain. It was so unfair. Why couldn't she just be normal?

Tara snuggled closer to the dog, closed her aching eyes and began the long wait for morning.

At breakfast, she tried to force down some cereal and a cup of coffee. She didn't even like coffee but needed some form of chemical help to get through today. Luckily, Mum was distracted, talking excitedly about a proposed shopping trip for her weekend away.

She didn't notice her daughter's red-rimmed eyes and the pale violet semi-circles beneath them.

At school the hours dragged slowly by until eventually the bell went to signify the end of the day.

Tara sagged with relief.

Mr Christos had told her off in biology for 'being dreamy' and she'd noticed Karis watching her a couple of times, but she'd somehow battled the dizzy nausea and stinging eyes of her terrible night. Stumbling towards the school gate, she looked at her phone and saw that a text from Leo had come earlier.

C U soon?

A pleasant warmth began to seep through her and then faded again. How could she possibly have a boyfriend and behave like anyone else when this was going on? Leo would dump her the minute he found out about it anyway. Was she really going to be able to keep it from him?

Miserably, she went to put the phone back in her bag without replying when it started to ring. The number ringing was unfamiliar and she realised it was the same person who'd tried her twice before. Persistent, whoever they were.

'Hello?' she said, holding the phone to her ear.

'Is that Tara?' The nasal voice made Tara's scalp prickle, even though it was unfamiliar.

'Um, yes, who's that?'

A pause. 'Tara, it's Siobhan Evans.'

Tara's footsteps came to an abrupt stop. Someone crashed into her from behind, stepping painfully on her heel.

'Watch out!' snapped a huge Sixth Form boy.

But Tara barely heard him. Her mouth went dry and her stomach lurched as though she had gone over a bump in the car at speed.

'Are you there? Tara?' said Siobhan.

'Yes.' Tara's throat felt so tight she could barely summon enough air to force the words out. 'What do you want?' she whispered. 'How did you get my number?'

'My cousin works in the office at your school,' said Siobhan. 'Your old one, I mean. She got it off one of your mates.'

Anger surged up inside her. Wasn't there supposed to be confidentiality about stuff like that? And what did Siobhan Evans want? To torture Tara a bit more about what she'd done?

'Why are you ringing me?' Tara marched across the road in the opposite direction to the flow of students leaving the school.

'Look, I know it's a bit of a surprise, me getting in touch,' said Siobhan with staggering understatement, 'but I'm visiting down the road from you. And I wanted to . . . see you. Can you meet me?'

'No!' gasped Tara. The very thought filled her with horror. 'There's nothing to say. I already said I was sorry. I'm more sorry than you can ever know.' Her voice hitched on the words.

'No, no, I know that,' said Siobhan, more gently. 'I really don't want to have a go at you, Tara. There's something I need to say. I'd sooner do it in person though.'

'I can't.' Tara was almost surprised at her own strength now. 'I'm really sorry, but I . . . I just can't. Say whatever it is now. Please.' *And then leave me alone*, she added in her mind.

Siobhan sighed. 'Well, okay, if it has to be like this,' she said. 'The thing is,' she went on, 'it's been on my conscience and I feel bad. Some harsh things were said about you and, um, some of them harsh things were said by me. I blamed you, you see.'

Tara squeezed her eyes tight shut at these words. Siobhan made a sucking sound and Tara pictured the cigarette clamped between her thin lips. 'I know you was only trying to help.'

Tara remained silent, listening hard despite the desire to fling down the phone and run away from Siobhan's words.

There was another long pause.

'The thing is, something has come up and I felt you

should know. It's been on my conscience, as I said.'

Tara's whole being focused around the voice that came into her ear.

'What has?' She spoke so quietly, she wasn't sure if Siobhan even heard.

'The thing is,' Siobhan repeated, 'the police came to see me last week. Said what they had to tell me was confidential. But sod that for a game of soldiers. I think you have a right to know. And it's going to come out soon anyway. Bound to, innit?' She sucked on her cigarette again, as though drawing in courage. 'Anyway, this woman went down the station. Said she was planning to steal . . . a baby.' Siobhan coughed before speaking again. 'She's cracked, from what I could tell. Lost her own kid a few years back. Anyway, the thing is, she confessed it was her what took my Tyler.'

Siobhan's composure crumbled. Tara listened to the snuffles on the other end of the phone. After a few moments, Siobhan spoke again, her voice bunged up and thick.

'Had him for a day but he got away, clever little bugger,' she said and gave a high-pitched sob-laugh. 'Tried to come home and that must have been when he got into difficulties.' Her voice skidded to a squcak at the end of the sentence. Some loud nose blowing followed, amplified by the phone so Tara had to hold it back from her ear for a moment or two.

Tara squeezed her eyes shut. She didn't want all these details.

'Look, Siobhan, I'm sorry but really it's nothing to do w—'

Siobhan cut across her.

'Tara, listen to me. That woman . . . her husband is a *stone mason.*'

'What?'

'Her hubby,' Siobhan pressed on, 'he makes statues and whatnot for graveyards. The police think she kept my Tyler in the workshop for the twenty-four hours he was missing. So,' she said emphatically, 'don't you see, Tara? Do you understand? It means you were right all along. You were right about those statues.'

Tara didn't notice much around her as she walked home. One foot went in front of the other and after some time, her house came into view. She managed not to step out in front of any buses or cars, but that was more down to luck than the attention she paid to her surroundings.

'You were right about those statues.'

The words repeated inside her head over and over again. When she got to her house, she fumbled with her keys and then Beck opened the door, a doorstep sandwich in his hand.

'What's up?' he said but Tara pushed past him.

'Gonna be sick,' she said, running towards the bathroom.

'Oh. Right-oh. I'll leave you to it then.'

Once inside the safe cocoon of home, the nausea subsided.

But when she sat down on the lid of the toilet, she began to shake so hard that her teeth chattered. She was icy cold and a pulse throbbed with a steady beat in her temple.

Leaning forwards, she rested her head in her hands, her elbows on her knees. Emotions churned inside her. She couldn't think straight. How was she supposed to react to this news from Siobhan Evans? Be grateful? Be relieved? She didn't know what she was supposed to feel. It was too complicated to feel any one emotion.

Tara got up and ran water into the sink. She threw some over her face and then dabbed it dry, looking at her reflection. A washed-out girl, skin the colour of porridge, looked back at her. The whites of her eyes were tinged with pink. Her hair hung inky-black against the pale oval of her face. How could Leo ever have been interested? She looked like a ghost. But even thoughts of Leo couldn't distract her from what she had just learnt.

Oh my God . . .

Those pictures . . . they weren't from a graveyard at all. They were from the stone mason's workshop. Like Siobhan said, she'd been *right*.

A smile crept over her face. She couldn't help it. A sort of savage pleasure mixed with fury welled up inside and she began to laugh. She couldn't stop. She laughed and laughed, quietly and then turning the taps on full blast to drown the sound as the laughter got more hysterical, her control loosening and slipping in a way that was liberating and frightening all at once. She didn't know where the tipping point came but now she was sobbing into the hand towel, shoulders violently heaving. She felt as though she would never be able to stop crying.

A knock on the door brought her back to her senses with a jolt.

'What?' She sounded as though she had the world's worst cold now.

'You still barfing? Want me to call Mum?'

Yes, yes, yes, she thought. *I want Mum and I want Dad and I even want insensitive YOU, Beck. I want all three of you to hug me and tell me it's all going to be all right. I want my family to make it go away. I don't want this. I don't want it. I don't want it . . .*

'Tar?'

'No, I'm all right!' she called thickly. 'There's no need.'

There was a pause.

'Tar?' Beck repeated.

'*What?*'

'You haven't got yourself knocked up, have you?'

Tara gave a tired sort of laugh. 'No, Beck. I haven't *got myself* knocked up.' How typical for a boy to put it like that.

'Okay . . . well, I'll leave you to it then.'

Tara sighed and stared at her reflection again. The evening with Leo at the pool felt like something from another lifetime. What was she supposed to do now?

Because if she had been right about Tyler Evans, that meant only one thing.

She was right about Melodie.

CHAPTER 12

SACRIFICE

Tara convinced her parents she had a stomach bug and spent the evening in her room, curtains drawn like a weak barricade against the outside world. She picked up her mobile to text Leo about five times but each time the necessary combination of words failed her and she threw it down again with a frustrated growl. What could she say to him?

Hello, I think your sister is in terrible danger. A man with a knife is cutting her and says you have till Friday before he does it again. Okay?

She tried to work it all through in her mind. What did they want? A ransom? But if Melodie had been kidnapped, how could Leo not know if this was happening? Wouldn't it even be on the news? Maybe the police hadn't been called. And maybe Leo didn't even know. Which raised the big question: was it Tara's job to tell him?

Perhaps those images might help track her down. Save her *life*, even.

All these thoughts ultimately led back to one place though. Leo finding out that Tara wasn't who he thought she was. She wasn't just an all-right-looking girl who liked a swim. Instead, she was a freak who saw freaky pictures in her freaky mind.

Tara squeezed her nails into the palms of her hands as she pictured the confusion and then the distaste in Leo's eyes. She knew she had to do it.

Tyler Evans was dead. Tara couldn't help him any more.

But Melodie didn't have to die too.

She, Tara, might be the only person who could save her.

At ten-thirty p.m. she snatched up the phone, and brought up Leo's name. Hesitating for a second she jabbed the call icon with a shaking fingertip. Her heart beat hard as it rang once, twice. And then she heard his voice.

'It's Leo.'

'Oh, uh, hi it's Tara, I . . .'

But the voice continued. 'Leave me a message and I'll call you back.'

She hung up. This was something she was going to have to do in person.

In the morning, Tara debated staying off school but Mum was home today and she knew she'd never get out of the house. She had to somehow put one foot in front of the other, getting through to half three when she could go to the pool and find Leo. What she would say when she got there was anyone's guess.

The temperature was cruelly high today. Everyone wilted, even Jada and Chloe who usually never broke sweat. But today, people gave little puffs of distress as they sank onto the grass, fanning themselves with books and magazines. The boys threw bottles of water over each other's heads and then shook like dogs.

Two almost sleepless nights had taken their toll on Tara. When three-thirty finally came, she went into the girls' toilets and slapped on more make-up than she would normally wear in an attempt to hide her pallor. But the mascara and kohl only seemed to accentuate the puffiness of her eyes. Dabbing bronzer onto her cheeks with a soft brush, she decided she looked like a clown that was coming off heroin. She tried to rub off the bronzer and her delicate skin reacted angrily, a rash spreading quickly across her cheeks. Tara sighed and regarded the reflection of her sorry self. Chloe walked in then and smirked at her in the mirror. Tara gave her an evil look and pushed past her to leave.

When she finally got to the park she sat on a bench and

ran over what she was going to say to Leo. Every time she thought she was sure of her script, she was seized with certainty that it sounded quite mad.

Finally, knowing she could put it off no longer, she dragged herself, miserably, towards the entrance of the lido.

Cassie was taking tickets today, looking pink-cheeked and shiny, blond hair pasted to her neck. She smiled vaguely at Tara as she took her ticket. The shouting and splashing coming from the pool were the loudest Tara had ever heard there. It felt all wrong.

'Sounds busy,' she muttered and Cassie grimaced.

'You're telling me,' she said. 'There are *millions* of kids today. Dave's almost combusting. Had to call in his grandson as a temporary lifeguard. He's not used to more than three people swimming. I told him he might have to get his trunks on and actually do some lifeguarding. You should have seen his face.'

Tara gave a weak laugh.

'Leo in?' she said, trying to sound light.

Cassie met her eye and nodded, a slight smile on her lips. Whatever Cassie was thinking, Tara wished she could stay here with her longer, chatting. She didn't really want to see him, not today. Heart leaden with the responsibility of what she had to do, she pushed through the barrier into the pool area.

And that was when she realised the situation was much, much worse than she'd anticipated. It wasn't only little kids and mums here today.

On the nearest patch of grass to the water, laid out on towels and facing the sun like sacrifices, were Jada, Chloe and a girl she didn't recognise with curly dark hair.

They all wore tiny bikinis, each girl lying as though waiting for a photo-shoot. For a split second Tara considered turning the other way. She hovered, undecided, when she heard someone say, 'Oh, hi,' cautiously. It was Karis, carrying a swimming bag, her hair in a long ponytail.

Tara sighed internally. Too late to back out now.

Karis regarded her curiously. 'Going for a swim then?' she said, flicking a curious glance over Tara. It was obvious she didn't have any swimming gear with her.

'Uh, no,' said Tara. Karis's eyebrows lifted and Tara stared back at her, expressionless. She didn't mind Karis really – she was certainly better than the rest of her bitchy crowd – but Tara simply couldn't think what to say. All her mental energy was taken up with the conversation she must have with Leo.

Karis's face closed off and she said, 'Right, well . . .' in a tight, unfriendly voice before moving away.

Tara felt a stab of regret but forced the feeling away.

Squinting against the bright glare radiating off the water, she looked for Leo. He was at the other end of the pool, squatting on his haunches and talking to some boys who must have been mucking about in the deep end, a stern expression on his face. Her legs and stomach instantly went all warm and liquidy, despite the weird circumstances.

But then she glanced back at Jada's crowd and saw that Chloe had her head up like a meerkat, clearly noticing her for the first time. She said something to the others. Jada sat up, grazed Tara with her look and then flopped back onto her towel. She heard the low, mean hiss of their laughter. Chloe actually drummed her heels against the ground as she laughed.

A lanky boy with spots and a shaved head was on the lifeguard's chair at the other end of the pool, studying his phone. Tara presumed he was Dobby's grandson.

Sunlight glanced off the water in an acid-bright glare. The relentless heat pressed down on her face. And Tara could still feel the eyes of the girls from school on her, although she didn't look at them. She'd never have believed it was possible to feel self-conscious about being fully dressed. There was bare skin everywhere she looked, while she was being mummified by the suffocating heat of her school uniform.

Leo still hadn't seen her as he began walking back along the pool. Then he glanced over and Tara could see the small grin that wrapped itself around his lips.

Jada sat up bolt upright now and stared at Tara with her lips slightly open. She beckoned to Leo as he passed, swinging her legs round to make room and patting the sun lounger. Tara couldn't hear the conversation against the background din but she could tell Leo was resisting sitting down. But Jada was insistent. Tara saw the white flash of her teeth as she beamed at Leo, reaching up to give a playful tug on his hand. In a second Tara understood that they had a history and felt a spasm of pure hatred for Jada.

Leo sat down. After a moment they both looked round at Tara. Dread crept through her. What were they talking about?

Tara desperately wanted to run away and not come back. Then she remembered the knife and the blood. And Siobhan Evans saying, 'You were *right*, Tara.'

Leo walked towards her now. His expression was unreadable. He wasn't smiling. Tara's stomach flip-flopped again but this time it wasn't with desire but nerves.

'Hey,' said Tara.

'Hey,' he said quietly.

'Have you got a minute?' Tara continued nervously. 'I need to talk to you about something.' It felt like she was talking to a total stranger.

Leo gestured at the pool. 'You can see what it's like today.'

'Please,' said Tara miserably. 'It's important.'

It was already over, whatever they'd had. She could tell. His whole manner was different, as though there was a glass barrier between them. It seemed impossible that they'd ever shared kisses. That she'd ever been close up to the face that now looked hard and cold.

Leo looked at his watch. 'Okay, five minutes or Dobby will have my balls on a plate.'

He led her into the cramped office back towards reception. It was stiflingly hot, and smelt of stale bodies and dampness. Leo cleared a chair for Tara and then leant back against the desk, arms folded. The distance between them seemed huge, even though it couldn't have been more than a metre.

'Why are you being so weird?' Tara hadn't really meant to start with this. The words came before she could stop them.

Leo scratched the back of his neck, frowning deeply. 'I don't know, Tara,' he said. 'You tell me.'

Tara's skin chilled, despite the heat in the room. 'What do you mean?'

'I'm not sure you've been all that straight with me, is all.' He paused. 'Why did you pretend to be friends with Mel?'

Flushing, Tara looked at the wall beyond Leo's head. 'I, uh, I . . .' she faltered.

'That's what I'm wondering,' continued Leo in a louder voice. 'I asked Jada if she'd got the message about Mel, yeah? And she was a bit surprised, wasn't she? Said you were never friends. In fact, she said you were a bit obsessed with her. Bit creepy, is how she put it.'

Tara sucked in her breath, truly shocked that Jada could say something so evil. *She wants Leo for herself*, was her next thought.

'Was it the famous dad thing?' Leo wasn't giving her room to speak, even if she had been able to find words. 'Did you think a bit of the old celeb lifestyle would rub off? Because you wouldn't be the first.'

'God, no!' said Tara, a response bursting from her at last. 'You've got it so wrong!' She ran her hands helplessly over her head and blew air out through her lips in frustration. 'Okay,' she continued, voice shaking, 'I *did* lie about knowing her. But there was a reason and it's nothing like what *you're* thinking!'

Leo frowned. 'What then? Go on, explain.'

Tara's breath caught in her throat. Where could she possibly begin? All the words she'd practised piled up inside, choking her.

Leo shifted and looked at his watch in a pointed way. It was rude. He was being horrible. But he was angry. He didn't understand any of it.

'Look, I've only got a minute,' he said wearily. 'I can't really —'

'*She . . . she's in danger!*'

Tara had finally let out the horrible thing in her head. The world could end now.

Leo stared as though she had spoken gibberish and then gave a short, weird laugh.

'What are you on about?' he said.

Tara wanted to turn away from the harshness of his expression, but she forced herself to levelly meet his eyes.

'Melodie. She's in serious trouble.'

'How do you know?' said Leo, a bit sneerily. Tara briefly wondered how he could ever have wanted to kiss her. He looked as if he didn't even like her now. She wasn't even sure she liked him that much either.

'I just . . . know,' she said, forcing herself to continue. 'I think you should get in touch. Whatever you think about me, and you're wrong by the way, whatever Jada told you . . . is so wrong . . . but you should find out what's happening with Melodie. It's really important. She needs you, Leo.' She bit her lip, hating the prickle of tears in her eyes.

Leo stared at her for an interminable amount of time. 'You're quite a strange girl, d'you know that?' he said.

'Yeah,' said Tara glumly. 'Believe me, I know.'

Freak . . .

She turned to go but Leo moved quickly and stood in front of her, barring her exit.

'Wait,' he said. 'You think we're *done*? You come here with some weird story about Mel being in danger and I get no explanation at all?'

'Please, Leo . . .'

'No,' he said tightly, his eyes hard and angry. 'You don't get to do that. Tell me what you know. It's about Will, isn't it? You looked weird when you brought him up that time. Like there was something you weren't telling me. Have you been seeing him behind Mel's back? Before he had that accident?'

'What? No!' Tara was unable to completely quash the small thrill that Leo cared. Maybe that was why he was being so horrible. Or maybe it was only because she was, as he put it, a strange girl. A girl who'd just told him his sister was in danger.

'It's nothing like that! And you won't believe me if I tell you anyway.'

'Try me,' said Leo. A shadow passed over the open window behind him.

'I get these ... pictures,' said Tara, almost whispering. 'When things get . . . lost. Keys, wallets, whatever. Ever since I was small. I kind of see where they are. I, um, know where to find them.'

'*See where they are?*' repeated Leo. He looked like he was struggling to understand something very complicated. 'See them how?'

'In my head. In my mind,' said Tara. Her cheeks throbbed with hot blood. 'But it's not only objects. I get pictures when people are missing too ... sometimes.' She took a deep breath and then forced herself to unpick words from the tight knot inside. 'I found something belonging to Melodie at school. And when I touched it, I got these pictures in my head of her being somewhere dark. She's scared. There's someone there who wants to hurt her. Making threats . . .' She couldn't make herself say the words, 'cutting her'.

She looked directly into Leo's face. Hating what she saw there, she pushed back her shoulders. She tried to think about self-respect and people who'd tried to take that away from her. People like Jay and the girls in her old school, when they found out about *Tara the Freak*. People like Jada and Chloe. She wouldn't let Leo do that. She'd never asked to be like this. It wasn't her fault. It was a curse. No one understood what it was like to be her. No one in the world.

'I've told you everything I know,' she said, suddenly tired of being here. 'You can go and snog your darling Jada now and then you can all have a good laugh at me.

But right now I want you to get out of the way because I'm going home.'

'No, you're wro—'

'GET OUT OF MY WAY, LEO!'

Leo stood to one side. Tara wrenched open the door of the office and almost knocked someone over who had been standing right outside. Jada. She had clearly been listening to every word of the conversation.

Her bottom lip hung open idiotically. And then her expression changed. A slow smile spread over her face.

Tara gasped at the malice glittering in Jada's eyes.

And ran.

CHAPTER 13

TING

The clock radio buzzed and Tara turned her groggy gaze to it. She hadn't expected to sleep at all but somehow it was seven-fifteen.

Friday morning.

YOU HAVE TILL FRIDAY THEN WE'LL CUT HER SOME MORE.

Tara tried to shake the thought from her head, groaning at the bright light coming through the curtains. She'd done her bit. And what a price she'd paid.

The last thing she remembered was lying in bed staring up at the ceiling, replaying the horrible look on Leo's face over and over again in her mind. It wasn't a look she was going to be able to forget in a hurry. The new, wonderful thing between them had been stamped on. It was gone.

And what about Jada? Tara's insides clenched as she remembered the expression on the other girl's face. Would losing Leo be the only price she'd have to pay?

She sorely wished she could hide in her bedroom all day but it wasn't an option. Mum was about, getting ready for her trip away and Tara knew that she would cancel it if she said she was ill. They were both looking forward to it so much.

She got up and forced herself to smile and nod in all the right places. Mum fussed about locking up and feeding Sammie and generally worried about Tara getting slaughtered in her bed or burning down the house.

'Anyway, Beck will be here,' she kept saying nervously. But Beck had whispered to her that he was planning a lads' poker night tonight round at a mate's. And then it was another mate's eighteenth birthday night at a club on Saturday. Tara doubted she would see him at all the entire weekend and that suited her fine. All she wanted to do was curl up with Sammie and watch mindless television until the rest of the world ebbed away. She only had to get through today first.

The memory of Leo's face as she'd told him about the pictures was seared onto her mind like a brand. His confused expression was so, so much worse than she had anticipated. He'd almost looked . . . scared. But scared of Tara, rather than fearful for Melodie. What boy wanted someone who freaked them out? None.

Tara dragged herself miserably through the morning, feeling like she had sandbags attached to her limbs.

At lunchtime she was walking distractedly towards the girls' toilets when she heard a stifled giggle. She spun round to see Jada, Chloe and the dark-haired girl from the pool. Molly. That was her name, she remembered now. They all had gypsy-style headscarves tied around their hair. Jada started to roll her eyes back into their sockets, her hands stretched out in front of her.

'I get these . . . pictures,' Jada screeched. 'Oh, I'm getting one now! Come to meeee, spirits!' The other two collapsed into liquid giggles next to her. Chloe crossed her legs like she might pee herself with hysteria. A group of younger kids was watching the display in slack-jawed admiration. Pierced by an embarrassment so acute she wanted to curl up and die, Tara rolled her eyes as though they all bored her.

'Oh grow up, you stupid bunch of cows,' she said and hurried away, hearing their laughter reverberating behind her. Tears pricked her eyes as she pushed open the doors at the end of the corridor and flung herself outside.

She numbly got through the rest of the day, avoiding looking at anyone if she could help it. At three-thirty she went to her locker. Her footsteps slowed when she saw that something was stuck to the door.

A piece of white A4 had been haphazardly taped there. The words *DO YOU SEE DEAD PEOPLE?* were scrawled in red pen. Underneath, like an afterthought, someone had written *Nutjob!!!!!* in blue felt-tip. Ripping the paper off the locker, Tara stuffed it into a bin, wishing she could run away, anywhere.

Bitches.

They didn't even seem to care about Melodie any more. They'd moved on after a couple of days of attention-seeking drama. They had a set of facts that worked for them: Melodie was okay and living in Brighton. They weren't going to budge from that position because some mad girl said they should.

Tara wished passionately that she'd never heard of Melodie Stone in the first place. Never come to live in this town.

Never met Leo.

As she walked through the school gates, she glanced at the other students around her. Those in groups or pairs were laughing or having earnest discussions. Others walked alone, pushing in earbuds and tuning out the rest of the world as they eased into their own space.

She envied every single one of them, whoever they were, whatever private problems they had in their own lives. She'd swap with any of them in a heartbeat.

Walking slowly home, she kept her tired eyes lowered. Her head throbbed. Every shout or flash of sunshine on a window felt like an assault. And pictures of cold steel biting into soft, white flesh had been on the edge of her consciousness ever since she had woken up.

She knew she should be trying to help Melodie somehow. But what could she do?

Leo didn't believe her. He thought she was unhinged. Worse, he thought she was some kind of stalker.

Sod you then, Leo, she thought, squeezing her hands into fists so her nails bit hard. You can get lost.

Then she had a vivid memory of the exact moment at the lido when he'd kissed her. She remembered the salt on his lips and warm hand on the side of her face. The slightly shy, wary look in his brown eyes and then the way his face relaxed into a smile. Like he was letting her in. Her and no one else. It made her feel special. Privileged.

There was no use pretending she didn't care. This *hurt*.

Tara's shoulders began to shake and the tears she'd been holding back all day finally came. She stumbled towards an alleyway by some shops and tucked herself away from any curious eyes. Leaning against the wall, arms wrapped around her middle, she tipped forwards and cried and cried until she ran out of tears.

Finally, worn out, she found a tissue in her pocket and tried to wipe away all the smudges under her eyes. She blew her nose loudly, trying to talk herself back up.

She'd get over it.

She'd been here before, hadn't she? She'd *get over it*.

But as soon as she had that thought she knew it was only a hollow wish.

This was *nothing* like what had happened with Jay bloody Burns. She felt a thousand years older than she was then. A thousand times wearier.

A thousand times . . . more in love?

Tara made a sound like someone had kicked her and covered her face with her hands. She wanted to scream until her throat bled. This was all wrong. But she knew she was falling in love with Leo and there was nothing she could do about it. Anything she'd felt before, for Jay, for boys she'd had crushes on . . . well, there was no comparison with this.

Leo was different. All of it was different.

And she'd lost him already. She'd had a glimpse of something amazing and now it was gone. Like someone had snuffed out a candle.

Maybe she wasn't allowed these normal things. Was that it? She saw things. But she wasn't allowed to be normal. Maybe this was the flipside of her so-called gift . . .

Gift? Tara gave a bitter laugh. That was a joke. She would do literally anything to be free of it. If she could cut it out of herself she would. She didn't want any part of it. She'd never asked for it.

Eventually, when the walls seemed to be closing in around her, Tara emerged from the alleyway and walked slowly home.

She was halfway there when her phone rang. She flinched, surprised, and pulled it from her bag.

Looking at the caller display she gasped.

Leo.

Frozen to the spot by indecision, Tara stared at the phone until it stopped ringing. Two seconds later, it started up again and she flinched, stupidly, a second time.

With a shaky hand, she held the phone to her ear.

'Hello.' Her voice wasn't much more than a whisper.

She could hear him breathing on the other end.

'Can I see you?'

'Why?' She squeezed her eyes tightly closed against a wave of longing and hope. She had to squash that feeling down. There was only so much humiliation a person could take. Thank God he didn't really know what she felt. At least . . . not the true extent of it, anyway.

A pause. 'I need to see you. Please, Tara.'

She silently let out a long slow breath. 'Where?' she said eventually, her resolve dissolving instantly.

'Where are you now?'

She looked around for the name of the road. He knew it. They arranged to meet in a playground nearby in ten minutes.

Tara's insides churned as she made her way there, wondering what he wanted. She didn't dare allow any hope to grow inside. Once at the playground she saw the benches Leo had told her about. Sitting down, she wasn't able to resist a quick look at her reflection in the screen of her phone. Knowing she looked like hell, Tara tried to tidy her hair a bit. There was nothing she could do about the puffy eyes and red nose.

She sat back and forced herself to breathe slowly. There were a few mums on the benches opposite and young children shrieked and called out from the slides and roundabout.

I'm not going to think about you, Tyler Evans, she

thought, as he nudged his way into her mind. *Don't you think I have enough going on?*

A few minutes later Leo appeared at the entrance to the playground. He raised his hand and dropped his eyes as he made his way over. Tara's insides flip-flopped. Why did he have to look so gorgeous? He had on a green T-shirt today that emphasised the light caramel of his skin. His short, dark hair was messy, as though he'd just been rubbing his scalp. Tara felt a moment's actual fury at him for looking the way he did. It wasn't fair.

He came and sat down next to her. They faced the playground, not meeting eyes. There was a gap of a few centimetres between them on the bench. But it felt as wide and uncrossable as a motorway. Eventually, Leo broke the silence.

'That was a bit weird ... what you said yesterday.'

'I know that,' said Tara tightly. 'It wasn't exactly easy for me. I just thought I should tell you.'

Leo turned to her. She risked looking sideways. His eyes were intense, worried. She looked away, unable to handle his gaze. He paused for two, three seconds before speaking abruptly.

'The thing is, Melodie's been ... kidnapped.'

Tara sucked in her breath sharply, drawing her fingertips to her lips.

'But how did *you* know?' he continued, louder now. A bit aggressively. 'Do you know something? Because you have to tell me if you do.'

Tara winced at the hard jabs of his words. She shook

her head, more tears threatening behind her eyes. 'No, no, I told you. It's something that happens to me. I can't help it.' *Oh, God*, she thought. *I'm going to have to tell him about Tyler Evans now.*

But Leo was staring into the middle distance. He kept squeezing one of his hands into a fist as it lay on the faded black denim of his thigh.

'She never got to Brighton,' he said, quiet again. 'No one has seen her for over a week. She'd insisted on getting the train to Adam's, even though Faith offered to drive her. She called me and she called Faith, leaving messages to say she was there. Well, you know. I played it to you.'

He glanced at Tara and then away again. There was a pause. She didn't want to interrupt. She waited for him to speak again.

'And now Faith and Adam have both been sent these pictures of Mel . . . all tied up.' The words came out in a rush. He swallowed and Tara saw a bright sheen in his eyes. 'They want . . .' His voice cracked and he cleared his throat. 'They want money from Adam. Fifty grand. Have said that if they go to the police, they'll . . .' He swore and leapt to his feet, savagely running a hand across the top of his head, mussing his spiky hair further.

'Cut her,' whispered Tara. 'I know.'

They met eyes. His contained such a lost look that he suddenly seemed younger than seventeen. He sat down again.

'Can you tell me everything you . . . see? You know, when you get the pictures?'

Tara told him, aware for the first time that, really, there wasn't a lot of useful detail to pass on. A dark room. A single lightbulb. A cot bed. It wasn't much. She could tell Leo was disappointed. 'I don't know if maybe you could give me something of hers and I could try again?'

He blew air out slowly through his lips. 'Might be an idea. But I promised Faith I wouldn't tell anyone. She's going nuts over there. Thinks if it gets out . . . well, it could be worse for Mel. I'd have to think about how we could do that.'

'Will he pay up?' said Tara after a moment. 'Her dad?'

Leo shrugged.

He sat with his head bowed. His nearest hand was still clenching and opening like a reflex. It hurt Tara somewhere deep in her chest to see him in pain. Before she could stop herself, she gently placed her own hand over his. He turned his over and clung on tightly.

'Look, I didn't mean to make you feel bad yesterday,' he said. 'It was just a bit hard to take in, you know?'

'I know,' she said quietly. 'It's not something I usually tell people.'

'I won't go around shouting about it,' he said.

'You don't need to,' said Tara. She quickly told him about Jada and watched a look of cold dislike creep over his face.

He swore. 'She's such a stupid cow.'

Tara couldn't help the feeling of hope that bloomed now. And also annoyance. 'You believed her yesterday. I thought maybe you and her . . .'

Leo gave a short, bitter laugh. 'Yeah, in her mind maybe. She's been flirting with me since she was about twelve. No thanks. Never understood why Mel likes her,' he said. 'And I'm sorry I listened to her yesterday. She was insistent, you know? I shouldn't have paid any attention but she got to me. I got it into my head that you'd only noticed me because . . .' he paused and swallowed, looking away into the distance, ' . . . because of something to do with Mel.'

Tara's heart was thudding. Was that what had happened yesterday? He'd been . . . hurt? Because he liked her? It was no good trying to squash down that hope any more. It was seeping into her veins like a painkiller and an energy drink all in one.

'No. It was nothing like that,' she said. 'I don't even like Melodie.' She hadn't meant to say that. 'I'm sorry,' she squeaked, horrified. But to her amazement, Leo barked a short, shocked laugh. Turning to her, she saw amusement in his eyes again. Then it faded back into worry.

'No, I really am sorry,' said Tara. 'I didn't mean it like that. Just that . . . well, I had no weird stalky thing, or celeb worship thing going on, that's all.'

'That's okay,' said Leo. 'I know better than most what my sister can be like. That last time I saw her . . .' He swallowed again. 'When we rowed? She actually hit me! And all because I told her not to do anything stupid like running away with Will.'

Tara looked away, debating whether she should tell him she had been there. But no, she decided he didn't need to know everything.

Leo's face was grim again. He looked down at his hands. 'But I tell you what . . . I'd do anything to have her back, in my face, being a pain. Anything.'

His eyes glistened, and there was a short silence before he spoke again.

'Look, I'd better get off,' he said, getting to his feet. 'I want to get back over to Riverdale Rise to see if there's been any news. Got to square things with Dobby first.'

'Okay,' said Tara. Leo dipped his face down to hers and kissed her. She closed her eyes and let herself be taken away from everything for a few moments. She never thought this would happen again. It was impossible not to dance a little inside, despite everything.

He gave her a small smile, although his eyes were clouded by pain.

She smiled back. 'Will you text me later if there's news? Or if you want me to . . . you know, help in any way?'

'Yeah, course,' he said.

Tara stood up and wrapped her arms around his neck, giving him one final, hard kiss. 'She's going to be all right,' she whispered, looking into his dark blue eyes. He closed them for a second, as though making a wish.

'I really hope so,' he said. He said it so quietly that the words were mostly warm breath on her face.

Tara walked home slowly, mulling over all the complex emotions she was feeling. Maybe she hadn't lost Leo after all. She'd been so sure . . .

She had to keep pushing back little flutters of pleasure. It was wrong to be happy when something horrible was happening to his sister.

It was only when she got to the house that she remembered the entire rest of her family was away. She opened the door and went inside, her improved mood deflating again. Sammie bounded up for an enthusiastic welcome. Tara dropped to her knees and made a big fuss, trying to stave off the emptiness of the house that seemed to wrap itself around her. The thought of being here alone all evening was horrible now. She even contemplated ringing Beck to ask if she could tag along to his poker party, but he wouldn't be keen. Well, she couldn't stay here, that was certain.

'Come on, boy,' she said and went to the cupboard to get the lead, which prompted a rapturous response from Sammie, who bounced at her with his wide doggy smile. She clipped on the lead and left the house.

It was cooler than she'd expected so she nipped back to get her cotton hoodie, slipping it on as they made their way down to the river. The Indian summer everyone had been on about seemed to be ending now. Trees along the riverbank had leaves tipped in gold and red. There was a distinctive autumnal smell from a bonfire somewhere. It made Tara vividly remember being a kid, when things like fireworks and Bonfire Night had seemed important.

She walked slowly, thinking about Leo and wondering whether there was any news on Melodie yet. She got out her phone a couple of times to check it hadn't rung without her realising it, even though she knew that was a bit daft when it was right there in her pocket.

She idly noticed people were up ahead. Tara recognised the woman and little girl on the bike she'd met that other time, the fateful evening when she'd seen Leo and Melodie fighting. What a lot had happened since then ...

The woman was calling out to the little girl, her back to Tara. Her body language transmitted impatience.

'Hattie, will you *hurry up?*' she said in an exasperated tone, walking backwards towards Tara. 'I told you we shouldn't bring the bike, didn't I? Didn't I say you were too tired after nursery?'

The little girl started to wail; her mouth pink and round with misery. She wasn't moving on the bike at all now. As Tara got closer, the woman turned to her and raised her eyes up, with a weak smile.

'Honestly!' she said. 'We'll be here all day.'

Tara smiled back sympathetically.

'I not coming!' yelled Hattie, crossing her arms, comically cross.

'Okay,' said her mother, catching Tara's eye and winking. 'That's fine, but *I'm* going to Nanna's for tea, even if you're not. Bye then!' She started to walk away.

The little girl's eyes widened. 'Mummeeee!' she cried out. Then with a look of grim determination, her chubby knees started to work the pedals and the bike trundled slowly forwards. She picked up speed and the bells tied to her handlebars tinkled. The little girl rode past Tara, shooting her a ridiculously grumpy look as she did so.

Ting, ting, ting, ting.

The little girl's mother turned. 'There's my big girl!' she called, grinning. 'Come on, you're going to beat me!' She pretended to run as the little girl speeded up.

Ting, ting, ting, ting.

Tara stopped walking. That sound . . .

What was it about that sound?

Adrenaline was coursing through her and her fingertips fizzed with energy. Why? *Why* did she feel like this? Something kept nudging the back of her mind, trying to make itself known. Something important . . .

But what *was* it?

Then, as though someone had pressed a switch and flooded a dark room with light, Tara understood.

The bells had reminded her of the wind chimes at Riverdale Rise. But she'd heard those wind chimes somewhere else recently. Heard them when they shouldn't have been there. When it came to her, an icy chill grasped her insides. The chimes had been there, ever so faintly, in the background of Leo's call from Melodie. The call that was meant to have come from Brighton. But she had actually been *at the house*, or right by it.

Tara started to feel excited. She didn't know what it meant, but it might be helpful. Melodie must have come back to the house for some reason. Why did she lie? Tara had no idea. Maybe she was going to sneak off to spend time with Will first? But she'd never got to see him, or he would have said so. Which may mean she wasn't far from home when she was snatched.

She had to tell Leo. Tara grabbed her phone and jabbed his number in with shaking fingers.

'It's Leo. Leave me a message and I'll call you back.'

Tara hung up. She didn't want to leave this as a message. There wasn't time. Those people could be hurting – *cutting* – Melodie right now. Even though the very thought made her feel sick with nerves, she knew what she had to do. She was going to have to force herself to go to the house and tell Faith directly. Even if it meant getting Leo into trouble for telling her. This wasn't about spooky 'gifts' or pictures. This was proper evidence; something she'd heard. They could hear too if he still had the message on his phone. Tara felt a surge of brave determination.

She hadn't been able to save Tyler Evans's life.

But maybe she could help save Melodie Stone's.

CHAPTER 14

SPIN

S he crossed the bridge and quickly found her way to Riverdale Rise. As she got close to the house, she hesitated. Sammie was a pain with new people and Tara didn't want the distraction of trying to stop him from jumping all over Faith. She could tie him to the railings at the far end of number ten's front garden. Mum wouldn't like her leaving him unattended but it would only be for a few minutes and, anyway, Faith probably wouldn't invite her in, not with everything that was going on.

Tara tied the dog's lead to the railings and he lay down with a sigh, dropping his head on his paws. Sammie regarded Tara sadly as she left him and approached the house.

She lifted the heavy door knocker and rapped twice.

There was no movement at all from inside. The house had an abandoned air. Tara shivered. She felt a bit sick and put it down to nerves. Or maybe she felt weird because this was Melodie's house and Tara was close to her things. Her chest tightened and she forced herself to take long, slow breaths.

Come on, she thought. *Hold it together, Tara . . .*

She rapped the door knocker again and this time could hear movement inside.

The door opened a crack. Faith peered out, blinking, as though the daylight hurt her eyes. She looked confused and then recognition crossed her face and she opened the door wider. Her eyes seemed large in her small, pretty face. She was shorter than Tara – doll-like in her floaty summer dress that showed off thin white legs. She seemed vulnerable and small and it gave Tara courage that she was doing the right thing. Imagine how Mum would feel if she, Tara, was the one missing? She *had* to try and help.

'Hello again,' said Faith in her soft voice. 'What is it you want, lovey?' Her slight smile didn't quite reach her eyes, which looked tired, the delicate skin beneath them almost translucent. 'Only I'm a bit busy right now.'

'Look, don't be cross with Leo, okay?' Tara blurted out, reflexively reaching out her hand. Faith looked at the hand curiously, as though it might be a dead fish, then up at Tara's face again. Tara started to blush furiously but hurried on. 'The thing is, I know what's going on . . . about Melodie.'

Faith's eyes widened. Her cheek twitched as though someone was yanking a piece of thread attached to it. 'What do you mean?' she said, her voice lower now.

'Leo, he, um, kind of told me,' said Tara with a spiralling sensation that things were happening too fast. 'We're . . .' She trailed off. What were they, exactly? All they'd done was kiss twice. She wished she could speak properly. And feel less odd.

She took a breath. 'Anyway the thing is that I heard a message on his phone and I realised something. I thought I should tell you in case it's important to help you find her . . .' Her voice trailed off. Faith was looking at her intently, her fair eyebrows drawn together.

Footsteps behind her on the street made Tara turn. An elderly man with a small West Highland terrier on a lead had stopped. He was looking at them with suspicion on his face.

'Evening, Ted,' said Faith, smiling sweetly. 'Can I help you with something?'

The man frowned and pulled his dog, which was stoically receiving Sammie's nose at its bottom.

'Well,' he said, 'I was just wondering whether you'd thought any more about tidying up this front garden,' he said stiffly. 'Only the Residents' Association and I, we think that —'

'Of course!' interrupted Faith brightly. 'I'll do it right

now, shall I? Alternatively,' she said, putting her finger to her cheek in a parody of deep thought, 'you could just *bugger right off and drop dead*!'

The man's eyes widened. Tara couldn't help but gape. The man opened and closed his mouth, fish-like.

'You'd better come in,' said Faith wearily, putting her small, warm hand on Tara's wrist. She drew her inside the house with surprising strength.

She closed the front door behind them and made an obscene gesture at the glass. 'Miserable old git,' she said. 'All he does is go on and *on*.'

Tara smiled back at her uncertainly.

'Why don't you tell me all about it?' Faith said. She walked along the hallway and down some steps at the end into another room. Tara hesitated. Her head began to spin a little. The black and white floor tiles of the hallway seemed to shift and blur as though the pattern in them was being re-set every few seconds. There was a star-shaped crack near her foot and the tiles were askew around it. Tara had to tell herself sternly not to trip, because she was dizzy enough to fall.

She pressed her hand to her chest as if she could slow her thudding heartbeat and picked her way around the bikes, boxes and piles of magazines in the hall. A ginger cat slunk in front of her, meowing in a piteous way. Another cat, a sleek Siamese, was curled up on the staircase to her left and it regarded her lazily through jade-green eyes. A wave of dizziness washed over her and Tara steadied herself by touching the long shelf that ran over a radiator running down the hallway. The shelf was cluttered with candles – some in wine bottles while others had melted in waxy stalactites over the side of the shelf. The air smelt of their sweet perfume and cigarette smoke with an undertang of cat. A pile of bedding with a pillow on the top was at the bottom of the stairs.

She followed Faith down the steps into a huge kitchen that led out onto the back garden. The kitchen was cluttered with newspapers, plates and cups on almost every surface.

A frying pan with congealing fat on the large Aga gave off a sour smell that caught in Tara's throat. Faith sat at the table and picked up a wine glass with a grainy red residue that was lying on its side. Tara's mind instantly filled with a picture of blood scabbing on skin and she blinked hard, trying to get rid of it.

Faith lit up a cigarette and blew smoke out sideways, regarding Tara with one eye slightly closed. She tapped her ash onto a large white dinner plate with a gold rim around it that was already crowded with cigarette butts.

'Sit down, darling. Sorry it's a mess, but . . .' Her voice wobbled and she wiped her eyes with the heel of her hand, her fingers curled inwards. 'It's a bad time right now.'

Tara nodded, feeling lost for words temporarily. She felt so sick . . .

Faith spoke again. 'Look, Leo really shouldn't have told you what's happening, you know. He could have made things bad for Mel. If it gets out . . .' Her eyes blurred with tears and she sucked savagely on her cigarette. Her face drifted in and out of focus and Tara blinked a couple of times.

Come on, she thought, *get it out and then you can go home and lie down . . .*

'It's okay . . .' She tried to breathe slowly. 'Please don't worry about me telling anyone. I promise I won't. And don't be angry with Leo. He's just scared.'

'Aren't we all?' said Faith, blowing a perfect smoke ring. Tara's stomach shuddered at the sharp smell. 'Anyway, what was it you wanted to tell me, sweet?'

Tara placed her hands flat on the table in an attempt to steady herself. It was sticky, so she withdrew them again and put them in her lap.

'Melodie left a message for Leo after she was meant to be in Brighton,' she said. 'Anyway, there was this noise in the background, really faintly. It was your wind chimes! She was *here* when she made that call. And she was all right then. At least, I think so. . .' Her words petered out.

Faith remained expressionless. She didn't even blink. Very slowly, she drew the cigarette up to her mouth and then seemed to change her mind, stubbing it out on the plate.

'Lots of people have wind chimes,' she said quietly, eyes cast down.

Tara frowned. 'Well, yeah,' she said, 'but you have, um, quite a lot, don't you? They're . . . noisy.' She blushed furiously. She hadn't meant to sound rude.

Faith nodded slowly. 'Yes, you're right. Thank you, Tara.

If we do call the police then this could be useful.' She looked up again. Her face was like a mask, her expression unreadable to Tara. Her eyes might as well have been holes for all the inkling they gave of what she was thinking. 'But it's very important you don't mention this,' she said quietly. 'Not to your parents, not anyone . . . Do you understand?'

'Yes, I promise,' said Tara in a small voice. A wave of nausea blasted her with heat.

'I feel a bit . . .' Her hand flew to her mouth. Her fingers were clammy and cold against her lips. 'Can I use your —' She was frightened to say more in case she was sick right there on the floor.

Faith gestured to the hallway. 'There's one down there on the right. Feel free.' She got up and went to the sink with the wine glass.

Tara hurried down the hallway and pushed open the first door on the right. It opened into a dark room. Tara fumbled for the light switch and her fingers found a rough cord hanging from the ceiling. She gave it a yank and strip lights buzzed and hummed into life. Wrong room. This was a garage, not the toilet.

Tara was about to turn the light off again when her body reacted to something before her mind could catch up. Her knees weakened and her heart punched against her ribcage.

She was looking at the single vehicle that filled most of the space in the garage. A van. A strong chemical smell made Tara's head swim sickeningly. A couple of spraypaint cans lay on the floor. The van had been sandpapered so that the original paintwork was patched and pale. The bonnet had been sprayed a different colour to the rest of the vehicle. The original colour showed through everywhere else in dull patches shaped like clouds.

It had originally been a white van.

A white van that someone was painting a new colour.

CHAPTER 15

SWIM

Tara seemed to glide down the steps without consciously moving her feet. She vaguely registered a door slamming somewhere and raised voices but was compelled to keep moving. Coming round to the front of the van, she ran her fingers over the crumpled dent there and pictured the solid, speeding mass of metal crunching into flesh and bone.

It could be a coincidence.

But she knew it wasn't. This was the van that had hit Will.

Shaking hard now, she peered into the van. A plastic sunflower was attached to the steering wheel. On the passenger seat lay a copy of *Grazia* magazine and a scrunched up cigarette packet.

This was *Faith's* van . . .

Had Faith deliberately run over Will?

Tara didn't know what it all meant, but she knew she needed to get out of there. She rushed back to the bottom of the stairs and then stopped abruptly. Icy horror flooded her veins. The door was open and Ross was standing at the top, filling the doorframe with his wide shoulders.

'What are you doing down there?' he said sharply.

'I was trying to find, to find, the loo, and I, I . . .' Tara couldn't seem to get her breath enough to force the words out. 'Sorry.'

She had to get out of here. Right now . . .

Ross stayed where he was in the doorway. Tara forced herself to keep moving upwards, meeting his eyes the whole way, daring him to stop her. To her astonishment, he stood to the side and let her back into the hall.

Relief filled every part of her body like pure oxygen as she hurried towards the front door, somehow managing not to run. Faith emerged from the kitchen and stared at Ross then Tara with a puzzled expression.

Ross put his big hand on her thin shoulder. 'Look, Fay, baby, it's all right. You have to let —'

'Shut *UP!*' hissed Faith, viciously shoving his hand away. She pushed past him and stood in front of Tara. Despite her small stature she seemed to fill Tara's vision now, monstrously big with blond hair framing a face that was twisted with fury. Her eyes bulged and Tara wondered fleetingly how she could ever have found Faith pretty.

Ross said, 'Baby, stop! This is not —'

And then everything happened very fast.

Faith's arm curved upwards, a dark green wine bottle clutched in her hand.

Tara just had time to think, *There's no way she would really hit me!* before blinding pain exploded in her head like a million fireworks.

Images swam and danced in her mind's eye.

Here was Beck as a little boy, crying because he'd skinned his knee.

Then Melodie's disembodied face loomed in before morphing into Faith's. She was yelling, soundlessly.

Here was Sammie, licking her face. *Urgh* . . . His tongue was so wet. It smelt so bad. Exactly like sick.

Consciousness began to seep back. Tara groaned. Her head pounded angrily and there was a sour wetness against her cheek. *She* had been sick. She was aware dimly of voices but couldn't open her sticky and heavy eyelids.

From somewhere she could hear a strange tinny voice.

'They're coming outta the walls! They're coming outta the goddamn walls!'

She knew that from somewhere . . .

Other voices began to penetrate the fog in her head.

'I'll call whoever it is back,' said a voice.

Leo? Leo was standing right outside that door!

'So you're still not going to call the police? I think you

have to do something.' His voice was a bit muffled but clear enough for her to hear what he was saying.

She wanted to cry out, to tell him she was here. Leo would make things better. And even though she couldn't exactly remember why, she knew something was very, very wrong. But Leo would help her.

'Leo!' she called out, her voice bright and strong. 'Leo! I'm here!'

Nothing happened. No one came to the door. The voices faded in and out.

Why wasn't he coming to help her? Then the sickening realisation hit her. She was only calling out in her head. She had to make her mouth work too. She tried again and a tiny croak emerged through her parched lips.

'L-e-o . . .'

But no one could hear her.

No one.

Tara tried to move but the pain was huge – a thing with a shape that sucked away all the light. Her eyes swam into focus. She was looking at the rough curve of a black, dusty tyre. The van. She was next to the van. The one that hit Will . . .

It all started to come back. Faith . . . the wine bottle . . .

Tara raised her limp arm and slapped the metal rim of the wheel but the sound wasn't loud enough. She needed something else. Moving her head slightly despite the pain, she spotted a spanner lying on the ground a few metres away and stretched for it. But it was too far. Voices were audible from the hall but she could only concentrate

186

on one thing at a time so they were indistinct, muted, like she was underwater. This thought gave her a weird burst of confidence. She was good in water. Tara the swimmer could do anything . . .

She slithered forwards a little on her belly like she was doing breaststroke on the hard, cold floor. Every movement punched at the pain in her head. Inch by agonising inch she moved until she was too winded to go further. Her fingers almost brushed the end of the spanner but she was still too far away to grasp it. Defeated, she gave a dry sob. She wanted to rest. Sleep until she felt better and it all went away. Beck's face came into her mind again then; he was laughing, tickling her until she screamed. Her brilliant, annoying, beautiful, infuriating brother. Would she ever see him again?

A flash of determination powered her to slither forwards another inch. Her fingers closed around the cold metal and she grasped the spanner, triumphant. Dragging herself back to the van, she banged the spanner against it. The harsh clang reverberated inside her head. The spanner felt so heavy. Too heavy. It spun out of her fingers and slid across the floor.

'What was that?'

'*Leo? I'm here, Leo!*' she gasped.

'It's that damn cat again,' said Faith in a high, clear voice. 'Keeps getting in the garage and knocking stuff down. Look, darling, there's no point in you hanging around here. I'm sure your father needs you home. I promise I'll call if there's any news, okay?'

The voices receded and Tara heard the sharp click of the front door.

Salty tears ran into her open mouth and then the world spun again.

CHAPTER 16

SHELL

The blackness began to dissolve. She tried to move her head but pain jack-hammered inside her skull and nausea gripped her stomach. Closing her eyes, she willed the sensations to pass.

Minutes went by. Or was it longer? Time didn't seem to run in a straight line any more but looped and rolled back on itself. When she opened her eyes again her bottom lip was smushed against something damp and cold. Raising her head and blinking heavy, sticky eyes she saw that she was lying on a duvet with a faded pattern of daisies and that she had been drooling on it. Coldness had seeped through the duvet from the hard floor beneath it.

Groaning, she forced her body up onto her elbows. Her head hurt everywhere, but one part of her scalp throbbed with bright urgency. She drew her tongue over dry lips, tasting blood; it felt swollen and oversized in her mouth.

She rolled onto her back and discovered her wrists and her ankles were bound with strong plastic ties. A single lightbulb hung in the middle of a ceiling above her, its glow sickly in the gloom. Familiar . . . but why?

A wooden chair, heaped with blankets, was opposite her. Then the blankets moved.

'*Are you awake?*'

The hissing voice kicked her heartbeat faster. She could see now that there was a figure there, sitting upright, hands folded between their knees.

'Well, are you?'

She hoped she was asleep. Then she would wake up in her own bedroom with sunlight soaking through her curtains.

But hot tears slid down her face because she knew this nightmare was really happening.

A waft of cigarette smoke pinched her nostrils, making nausea swell up again. A deep sigh came from across the room. The memories hurtled back into her mind.

Of course.

It was Faith who was there, watching her as she stubbed out a cigarette.

'Let me help you sit up,' she said now, in an irritable tone, as though Tara's prone form was inconveniencing her. When she crouched down and stretched out her arms,

Tara cowered from pure instinct, like a cornered animal.

Faith made a disgusted sound. 'Look, I didn't mean to hurt you,' she said. 'Don't be such a baby.'

She helped Tara into a sitting position against the wall. Tara watched her warily. Faith's breath smelt sour and her eyes had a blurriness to them. Tara realised she was drunk, but not so drunk that she wasn't in control.

Faith sat down on the chair again, drawing her thin, little girl legs under her, and adjusted the skirt of her dress demurely.

'What am I going to do with you, eh?' she said, drawing a pack of cigarettes from a pocket. She lit another one. Her eyes never left Tara's face.

'Why couldn't you just have minded your own business?' she said, in an oddly distant way. 'None of it has anything to do with you.' She contemplated Tara, top to toe. 'You're quite pretty but nothing special. I'm sure Leo could do better than *that*.'

This stung harder than it should have done. Tara quickly contemplated whether she could attempt to lunge at her, despite the bound hands and ankles. She, Tara, was so much bigger. But when she tried to move her legs, she found she was still kitten-weak.

She swallowed. Her lips felt dry and rough. 'Where's Melodie? What have you done to her?'

'I haven't *done* anything to her, you silly girl,' said Faith, one eye narrowed against a thin plume of smoke that curled up past her cheek. 'And as to where she is . . . she's over *there*, isn't she?'

191

She gestured vaguely to the right with her cigarette. Tara followed her gaze and then gasped.

Across from where she sat, in a space underneath a staircase, a daybed was tucked away. Tara could see the top of Melodie's head poking from under a duvet. Her distinctive hair, dull and greasy-looking now, lay scattered across a pillow. One arm flopped downwards to the floor, the fingers gently curled inwards. Drink cans and magazines littered the ground around her.

'What's wrong with her?' Tara's words came out as a gasp. 'What have you done?'

'I told you!' said Faith irritably. 'I haven't bloody done anything! She's a bit stressed that's all.' Faith blinked several times in quick succession, as though trying to clear unwanted mental pictures. 'I've given her some of my benzos so she can rest.' She caught Tara's puzzled look and actually laughed. 'You are an innocent little thing, aren't you? Benzo-diaz-e-pines,' she said as though she was talking to a child. 'To calm her down a bit.'

Tara's head throbbed. She closed her eyes for a second and then opened them again. Faith's outline blurred and then wobbled back into focus.

'I didn't want this to happen, you know, any of it. *Bloody* Adam!' Faith slapped her leg. 'None of it was supposed to get out of hand like this.'

Tara felt as though understanding was tantalisingly close, but she couldn't quite grasp it.

Faith swore repeatedly and then went silent. Then she

spoke again. 'He can afford it! He's loaded! And he's barely ever given us a penny. He's been no kind of father to Mel. It's time he paid his dues.'

Oh.

Tara got it, suddenly and absolutely.

'You *pretended* she'd been abducted?' Tara wished she could run as far and as fast as she could but, bound as she was, even standing up seemed impossible. Her limbs were as useless as if they were made of cotton wool. 'Does Leo know?' *Please, please say no.*

Faith sucked hard on her cigarette. The end glowed brightly, a warning light in the gloom. 'Of course he doesn't!' snapped Faith. 'Straight-laced old Leo? Give me a break. He's seventeen going on forty, that one.'

Thank God . . .

'This won't work,' said Tara hotly then. 'You have to let me go. You can't keep me here. My family will be looking for me.'

Faith rolled her eyes. 'Well, not straight away they won't. Lucky I've got your phone, eh?'

'*What?*'

'I've read your messages,' said Faith. 'Mummy and Daddy having a lovely lickle weekend away?' She used a horrible baby voice. 'So don't forget to feed the dog, will you? And lock up? Because you know what your brother's like, don't you?'

Tara caught her breath. Faith stood up suddenly and smoothed down her skirt.

'Don't worry, I've told them everything's fine, *Tabs,*'

she mocked. 'So you can be our guest for a little longer, can't you? Until I decide what the hell to do with you.'

She got up and walked up the stairs. The door banged closed and Tara heard the sickening click of the key turning in the lock.

Panic washed over her then and she thrashed and rocked, trying to free her hands. But the plastic ties only bit harder into her wrists and ankles. She sobbed wretchedly. Terror was making it hard to think straight but she knew she must. Surely Faith wouldn't . . . kill her? But she'd thought Faith wouldn't hit her over the head and look how that had gone. Judging by how bad she felt, Tara might have been lucky that blow hadn't finished her off.

She'd almost forgotten the reason she was here in the first place. With a jolt she looked across at the girl lying immobile on the day bed.

Faith said she'd drugged Melodie. Tara *had* to make her wake up.

'Melodie!' Tara hissed. 'MEL!'

But the other girl didn't stir.

Tara tried to get to her feet. She quickly discovered how very hard that was when your hands and ankles were tied, not to mention combined with the feeling that your head might split in two. She made it as far as her knees and then sank back with a frustrated groan. There was no way she was going to be able to walk anywhere.

Lifting her hands to her scalp she tentatively dabbed where it hurt most. There was a lump there, hard and curved like an egg. Vomit rose in her throat and she pulled her fingers away, looking down at the brown, crusty blood on them.

She tried calling Melodie's name again, louder, but got no response. Tara wondered how drugged up she was and looked around the dimly lit room, searching for anything she could use to cut the bindings. But there was nothing in here. It was a plain, gloomy box of a place with unplastered breeze-block walls, containing only the day bed, lamp and chair. Maybe a cellar? There was a familiar smell that might be coming from the river. But Tara's senses were muddied still by the blow to her head and she couldn't be sure of anything.

'MELODIE!' she screamed, surprising herself with her own volume.

There was a low moan and then Melodie slowly sat up. She looked at Tara with clouded eyes. Her hair hung over her face in greasy rat tails and she swiped it away with a thin, pale hand. Melodie's eyes widened as she seemed to see Tara properly for the first time.

'Thank God you're awake! You have to untie me!'

Melodie stared back at her, apparently dumbstruck.

'Am I dreaming?' she said in a thin, croaky voice.

'No, you're not sodding dreaming!' said Tara savagely. 'Now get over here and help me!' She held up her bound hands, suddenly enraged at Melodie for putting her into this situation in the first place. Some part of her felt it couldn't really be happening. Had she really been whacked over the head and tied up? Did that actually happen in real life? Well, it did, but not to people like Tara, surely?

Melodie swung her legs round slowly and got to her feet, looking about as stable on them as a newborn foal. She wobbled over to Tara, who held her hands higher. Melodie pulled and prodded uselessly at the ties around Tara's wrists.

'I can't,' she said, frowning as though trying to work out a complex problem. 'I don't really understand . . .'

'Well, you have to try,' snapped Tara, breathing heavily. 'There must be *something* we can use. Have you got scissors or a knife or anything?'

Melodie's eyes widened at the word 'knife'. She put her hand over her other upper arm as though it was a reflex. It was only then that Tara realised her arm was bandaged. Melodie's hoodie hung over it, the sleeve dangling uselessly. She couldn't make sense of what had happened here. Was Melodie a victim? Or was she part of the plan? There wasn't time to work any of it out. She had to get out of here.

'Look . . .' She tried to speak slowly and calmly. 'You have to help me. Do you understand?'

Melodie shook her head like a child. 'No, I don't. I don't understand. Why are you here?'

Tara could feel every last drop of patience ebbing away.

'I'll tell you why I'm here,' she said. 'Faith *hit* me. She hit me over the head with a wine bottle. You want to know why?' Her voice got louder. 'Yeah? I'll tell you, shall I? Because I found out the mad bitch ran over Will in her van. *And* I know all about the stupid kidnap scheme.'

Melodie stared at Tara. Her mouth was actually hanging open. She backed towards the cot bed and sat down, as though her legs wouldn't support her any longer.

'Will?' she said breathlessly. 'My Will? How do you even know *him*? And what do you mean about a van?'

Tara spat out her reply. 'Like I told you, *she* . . .' she pointed at the stairs, 'ran him over and put him in a coma. And I found out about all of it. So now I'm here too. Which is totally unfair!'

She struggled against the ties again with a wretched sob, but it was only then that she saw the effect her words had had on Melodie, and remembered that Will was Melodie's boyfriend. Melodie was gripping fistfuls of hair in a way that looked painful. Tears streamed down her cheeks and made shiny trails.

'Are you lying?' she squeaked. 'About Will? Why would you say that to me?'

Tara felt herself soften, guilt creeping in a little at how she'd delivered this news. 'Because he knew something had happened to you,' she said more gently. 'He was worried. He didn't believe you'd moved away with your dad.'

Melodie began to shake. 'I couldn't tell him!' she wailed. 'I wanted to! But I knew he wouldn't like it. And it was all going to be okay afterwards . . . We could pick up again and carry on.' She made a gulping sound. 'He's going to be all right though, isn't he?' Her face seemed to collapse in on itself, her small features distorted by grief.

'Probably,' said Tara, looking away. She had no idea.

She obviously hadn't been very convincing either. For several minutes Melodie sobbed in a quiet, defeated way. She didn't seem like the same person who flicked her hair and made nasty comments and generally swanned around like a queen bee. This Melodie had a gaunt face, greasy hair and shaking hands. She blinked constantly, like a creature that was used to living in the dark.

Tara stared down at the binding on her wrists, trying to think about how she could free herself. It was the sort of binding Mum and Dad used in the garden. It was strong. And every time she tried to wrestle it loose, it just bit further into her skin. Melodie was right too – there was nothing she could see down here that could be used to cut the ties.

Panic began to mount as Tara tried to assess her options. Maybe Beck would make an unplanned visit home and be worried? He'd ring Mum and Dad, who'd come back from their weekend away and call the police . . .

But Tara knew this wasn't going to happen really. Beck wouldn't know she wasn't at home until Sunday night when her parents returned. And if that mad woman upstairs was responding to Tara's texts, Mum and Dad would have no reason to worry.

Maybe Leo would realise something was wrong? But he had too much going on. His worries about his sister would be filling his thoughts, not Tara.

A sudden thought made her suck in her breath. *Sammie* . . . The poor dog was still tied up out there. Maybe he would howl and alert help? But even as she pictured it, Tara knew this was a pointless wish. The dog's collar wasn't that tight but even if he managed to get free, there was no reason why anyone would know Tara was here. The disloyal animal would go with whoever offered him food.

Her spirits were dropping further by the second. No one would know she was gone for two whole days. A lot could happen in that time. Faith seemed capable of anything. She looked over at Melodie, who lay across from her, silent apart from the odd hiccupping sob.

Tara felt another surge of anger towards her.

'Hey,' she said harshly.

Melodie slowly rolled round and sat up, drawing her knees to her chest.

'That hurt?' said Tara nodding at her bandaged arm.

Melodie looked down at herself. 'It's not too bad,' she said in a flat tone.

'As we're stuck here, you might as well help me understand what you were trying to do,' said Tara. 'It seems like we have time to kill.' Even as she said it, she winced inside at the word *kill*. 'So if you agreed to this,' she continued, 'how come they cut you?'

Melodie's lips trembled and she did a wet sniff, drawing her hand across her face. She would never have done anything like that before. It was as though the shell of the shiny, hard girl had been cracked open and Tara was seeing her raw insides.

'I didn't want them to do it . . .' said Melodie in a tiny voice, 'but Adam was threatening to go to the police. I don't even care about the money. Well, I do . . .' she said, a bit more firmly. 'I get an allowance from him but it's not that much really. He should definitely pay more.'

The little bit of sympathy Tara had been feeling drained away.

'So it's all about money,' she said disgustedly. 'You could all end up in prison for this, do you understand that? You actually let them *cut* you? Are you insane?'

Melodie looked away from Tara's harsh gaze. 'It had to seem realistic for the photo we sent him,' she said quietly. 'I didn't like being in here at first. I was scared . . . but I got used to that. And I drank loads of vodka before they . . . did it. I changed my mind when the time came but Faith persuaded me it had to be done . . . and Ross sort of held me down.' She sniffed again and drew herself up straighter. 'It was strictly a one-off anyway.'

'Oh you think?' said Tara sarcastically. 'Then why have they told your dad they'll do it again on Friday, which is today, FYI?'

Melodie's large eyes widened. 'You're lying,' she whispered.

'Okay, let's see then.'

Tara almost enjoyed saying this, even though it was cruel.

Then something occurred to her. Something so terrible that her guts corkscrewed inside her.

Maybe they wouldn't cut Melodie again. Maybe they would cut Tara instead . . .

If you couldn't see her face, one white girl's skin was going to look much like another's.

A barely perceptible moan escaped her lips and she dropped her head to her knees, curling into a ball like a small child who thinks they can't be seen that way. Nothing so far – not seeing the van, nor Faith coming at her with the bottle, nor waking up in that garage – none of it had scared her more than this. Waves of terror rolled over her and she began to shake so hard that her feet tapped against the cold stone floor uncontrollably.

Melodie didn't seem to notice her distress. Either that or she didn't care.

'I still don't understand what the hell any of this has to do with you,' Melodie said. There was a pause. 'What possible connection do you have with my family?' A beat passed. 'Oh I get it,' she said in a harder voice. 'Are you after Leo or something?' She laughed a mean, short laugh. The old her had been lurking there all along, it seemed. 'Well, I'd forget about that. He's out of your league, love.'

Tara didn't bother to answer. She was beyond being hurt by this. Melodie knew nothing about the kisses in the rain, or the way she'd felt when Leo wrapped his arms round her, enveloping her in his warm boy smell with its hint of chlorine. No one could take any of that away from her. But these precious memories weren't much use to her now.

She heard the sharp scratch of a match. Smoke wafted towards her in sickly curls.

'Do you have to smoke?' Tara said, her head snapping up. 'It's horrible in here and that just makes it worse.'

Something occurred to her then. 'And where are we, anyway? What is this place?'

Melodie blew smoke out the side of her mouth in exactly the same way that Faith had done it. What did Leo say before? Faith had more or less brought Melodie up. Tara suddenly wondered what it was like to have been looked after by that horror upstairs. Maybe it partly explained why Melodie was being such a bitch even now.

'The Bomb House.'

'*What?*' Tara thought she must have misheard.

Melodie sighed as though Tara was being particularly thick.

'That's what me and Leo called it when we were little. It's a whatchamacallit, bomb shelter from the Second World War. Faith's always wanted to turn it into a studio for her music, but we've never had the money.'

'Where is it?' said Tara sharply.

'Bottom of the garden.'

'I never saw anything there from across the river . . .'

Melodie made an irritated sound and sucked on her cigarette. 'Well, it's hidden by the weeping willow, isn't it? You can't see it from across the way.'

Melodie seemed quite recovered now as she sucked away on her fag. As though this entire crazy scene was normal. That was a scary thought. She needed Melodie on side.

'We have to get out of here, Melodie, do you understand that?'

'I'm not going anywhere,' said Melodie, gesturing with

her cigarette. 'And I'm sure Faith will let you go once Adam pays up.'

Tara gaped at the other girl. Did she really think Faith would just open the door and say, 'Bye bye, Tara, you can go home now'?

She was at least half as barking mad as her aunt.

Tara closed her eyes. She felt so weak . . . and her head hurt so much.

She must have drifted a little because when Melodie spoke again, she experienced a swooping sensation, like she'd been falling and only just managed to hang on to a ledge.

'Wha . . . what?' she said croakily.

Melodie was staring right at her, her arms around her knees. She'd put on a pair of fluffy Ugg-like slippers now and the duvet was around her shoulders. Tara realised how cold she was and tried to pull the duvet under her in the same way.

'I said,' Melodie repeated, '*you* don't know what it's like.'

'What what's like?'

'Not being wanted.' Melodie fiercely swiped the heel of her hand over her eyes. 'Have you got any idea what it's like seeing pictures of my dad with his shiny new family on the internet? There they are skiing . . . and, and, hanging out at theme parks in designer clothes.' Her voice wobbled. 'He dumped my mum and then he dumped me because I remind him of her too much. Do you know what that *feels* like, Tara Murray?'

Tara's mind filled with images of her family. Dad peering

at her over his reading glasses and then breaking into a twinkly grin. That time when she was little and convinced a monster lived under her bed and he'd pretended to do magic to make it go away. Then she thought of their Cornish holiday a couple of years ago. They'd all tried surfing and the one person who could do it, who was a total natural, was Mum. For weeks afterwards she'd break into a daft old surfing song and pretend to do it wherever they were, even if that was the middle of Tesco's. And Beck . . . She remembered him chasing her with the hosepipe in the old garden and his raucous, ruthless laughter at her shrieks. All these images had the rosy slow-motion quality of an old movie, of moments gone for ever.

An ache of longing for her family squeezed her heart.

No, she didn't have any idea what it must feel like for Melodie. She didn't know what to say.

Silence fell for some time before Melodie spoke again, less aggressively now.

'I still don't get it,' she said. 'How *did* you find out? Because Leo doesn't know anything about this. I can't work out how you knew I was here.'

Tara stared down at the stone floor. Should she tell her? She tried to work out what she had to lose. Everyone at school already knew. Leo knew. And she was currently being held captive by a pint-sized psycho. Preventing Melodie from knowing her secret didn't seem like much of a priority right now. She inhaled slowly.

'I found your earring at school,' she said at last in a low voice. This was an edited version of events. But Melodie didn't need to know about Tara looking in her locker. 'And I have this thing . . .'

'*Thing?*'

'Yes, thing!' sighed Tara. 'I see when stuff – and people – are lost or missing. And I saw you. In here.' She forced herself to meet Melodie's frowning gaze. 'I knew something was happening to you all along,' she continued. 'I knew you'd never gone to Brighton.'

A long silence stretched between the two girls. And then Melodie gave a huge, shuddering sigh.

'I don't even know what you're on about!' she said. 'I think you're a total freak!'

Incredibly, laughter bubbled up from somewhere inside Tara. It began to come in waves and then she found she couldn't stop. Hysteria rocked her so hard she thought she might laugh herself sick. Her stomach muscles ached and tears trailed down her dusty cheeks. 'You think I'm a freak?' she gasped when she regained the power of speech. 'Well, join the queue, *Melodie Stone*!'

Wiping her face and still giving little spurts of laughter, she only realised the door at the top of the stairs had opened when she saw Melodie staring upwards. Faith stood motionless there, her face with that creepy blank look again.

'What's happening?' said Melodie.

Faith didn't answer. She came down the stairs quickly, bare feet slapping against the stone. Her hand was behind her back and Tara couldn't see what she was holding. Her eyes didn't leave Melodie's face.

Melodie gasped and then began to cry softly.

'What's going on?' said Tara sharply but they both ignored her. Melodie slowly shook her head from side to side. Faith sat on the side of the bed next to her.

'No, no, no!' moaned Melodie quietly but she slumped into Faith's now open arms.

'Shh, shh,' crooned Faith, stroking Melodie's hair, rocking slowly with her. Tara's brain couldn't seem to make the necessary connections. What was happening?

Faith put her hands on either side of Melodie's face and looked into her eyes, still gently shushing her. Melodie cried unselfconsciously, a film of saliva stretching across her mouth that made Tara want to look away, but she couldn't move her eyes.

'I think he's really close to coming through for us, babes, okay?' said Faith in a low tone. 'And that's great! But we have to make him hurry up. Leo keeps ringing me. Ross is going on and *on* about us getting caught. We have to bring this to a close, yeah? D'you understand Mell-bells?'

'But it hurts . . .' wailed Melodie, her voice thin and high.

That was when Tara saw the glint of the sharp kitchen knife in Faith's hand.

And with a sickening rush she understood.

CHAPTER 17

CUT

You have until Friday . . .

'No!' Tara shouted, startling Faith and Melodie, who turned to her as one. 'You can't!' Tara tried to shuffle across the floor uselessly.

'Do it to *her* instead!' Melodie yelled.

Tara stopped dead, frozen to the spot with icy shock.

'But I was trying to help you . . .' she whispered. 'How could you?'

'Fay? Where are you, babes?' The deep voice barked into the space from the top of the stairs. Ross appeared. He peered into the gloom, frowning.

'Fay?' He sounded shaken, not at all cocky now. 'I'm

going nuts up here! We have to talk! What are you doing?'

'I'm *busy*,' said Faith, her voice a hiss of pure disgust. 'Can't it wait?'

'No!' Ross clattered down the staircase. He seemed to fill the small space with his male bulk. His eyes flicked to Tara and his features spasmed with something like pain. He lifted his hands to his face, making a rubbing motion outwards, like they were a pair of windscreen wipers.

'What do you want?' snapped Faith and she slowly lowered the hand holding the knife.

'It was on the radio,' he said in a shaking voice. 'That boy, Will, he . . .' Ross started to cry in ugly, gulping sobs. 'He's dead, Fay . . . He's bloody *dead*!'

Melodie made a sound like she'd been punctured. A thin high wail came from her mouth, which was stretched wide open. She wrapped her arms around her legs and rocked, head on her knees. Tara barely dared to breathe.

Faith got up, her face grimly set.

A torrent of words spewed from Ross. 'Don't you understand? This has got ten times worse. That's *murder*! You murdered that boy! I told you this had to stop, but you wouldn't listen, would you?' He gave a half-hysterical laugh. 'Oh no, Faith knows best. Faith says everything will "work out, baby, you'll see".' The false approximation of Faith's voice was uncannily accurate.

'Shut up!' snapped Faith, moving quickly towards him.

Ross came to the bottom of the steps. He took hold of her arms and looked into her eyes. She was crying now too.

'You know I love you,' he said quietly. 'Don't you? I really love you, Fay. But I never signed up for any of this.'

'Oh yeah?' said Faith viciously through her tears. 'You were just as into this idea as me. Don't pretend you weren't now, just because things have got a bit tricky.'

'A bit *tricky?*' yelled Ross, his voice booming. 'Is that what you call this mess? What about her?' He pointed wildly at Tara. 'You've got to let her go! It's all gone too far, sweetheart, can't you see?'

'That's why we have to follow through!' shouted Faith. 'It'll all be for nothing otherwise! We need to send another picture to Adam! And we don't even have to hurt Mel this time, don't you see?' She cocked her head at Tara.

Tara shuddered.

Ross stared down at Faith, his expression a mixture of love and disgust.

'No, baby. This ends now. I can't be part of this any more.' He turned to go back up the stairs, his broad shoulders slumped. Faith leapt after him.

'No, you can't! You'll ruin it all!' she screamed. Her arms went around Ross at a strange angle as though she was giving him an awkward hug.

Ross gasped and looked down at the blood flowering across the bottom of his white T-shirt.

'Fay?' he whispered, then toppled, crumpling forwards down the stairs. He landed heavily in a foetal position at the bottom.

Tara was hyperventilating. Panic squeezed her

airways. Her eyes kept filling with the awful scene in front of her.

Faith stared down at Ross. Her mouth hung slackly open. She made no sound at first, then a high-pitched keening split the air. Faith sank to her knees in front of Ross's prone body.

'I didn't mean it, babes!' she wailed, gulping between each word. 'I just wanted everyone to stop going on at me! Wake up! Wake up!' She pounded him with her small fists. His eyes were half open and gurgling sounds came from somewhere deep in his throat. Faith suddenly jumped back and ran back up the stairs, her thin legs like pistons. The door slammed and Tara heard the key turn in the lock again.

She shuffled with painstaking slowness to Ross, whose eyes were open now, staring and shocked. His left hand cupped his lower belly, where the blood was quickly spreading in a dark stain.

'What should I do?' she said. 'I don't know how to help you!'

She desperately tried to drag details from her brain about what to do when someone was bleeding. The only thing she could think of was to apply pressure. Blood was pooling at a frightening rate, forming a dark, sticky puddle on the floor. Tara managed to drag the duvet over to Ross and tried to shove it under his back. He groaned in agony.

'Sorry, sorry, sorry!' she squeaked. He was so heavy. She couldn't get her hands underneath. He did a barely perceptible rolling motion then and it was enough for her to push the corner of the duvet underneath him. Pulling it around the other side, she roughly wrapped the corners together, not tightly, but just so the stain on Ross's abdomen was covered by the bunched up duvet. It was the best she could do.

Ross was trying to say something.

'What?' She put her ear to his open lips. A bubble of blood appeared and then popped.

'Ocket . . .'

'What do you mean?' she begged. 'What are you trying to say?'

'*Ocket . . .*' Then his eyes closed and his face loosened. Tara put her cheek near his mouth. But there was no warmth there at all.

Oh my God.

Was he dead?

Terror kept surging over her in waves, making it hard to think straight, and then she realised what he had been saying.

Pocket . . .

Twisting awkwardly, she managed to slide one of her bound hands into the narrow pocket of his jeans. There was nothing there but some change. She tried the other one. Nothing. Then she reached into his back pocket and found some keys. There was a small penknife attachment there. Her heart leapt with hope.

Oh, thank you, thank you . . .

Her bound hands were shaking so violently that she dropped the keyring twice before she managed to pull out the small knife. Then she accidentally stabbed her wrist, drawing blood. But the pain meant nothing. She'd heard about soldiers running on broken legs in the heat of battle. When your life was in danger, cuts, bruises and broken bones didn't matter any more. She knew that now and wished passionately that it was still just a dry fact in a book.

It felt like she was awkwardly sawing at the plastic for hours. Finally, eventually, it snapped. She whimpered with relief. Cutting the ties on her ankles was easy after that and, once done, she got up and bounced on the spot for a minute to get her circulation going again. She shook her fingers as the feeling began to flood back in painful pins and needles.

Melodie hadn't spoken or moved throughout all this. She lay face down on her folded arms, her elbows jutting out to the sides. She was utterly still and quiet, almost as though she wasn't breathing. Tara looked away. From now on, it was every girl for herself. Melodie had showed her that.

Tara hurried up the stairs as fast as she could, almost dropping the keys on the way. There were only three on there and she fumbled with each one, putting it into the keyhole and trying to make the tiny mechanisms inside shift and comply by will alone. But none of the keys fitted the lock. Slapping the wood in fury, she began to moan. The damp, cold walls of the shelter seemed to pulse and close in around her.

Come on, she thought. *Calm down. You have to think . . .*

Tara had never tried to pick a door lock and didn't even know if it was possible in real life. She knelt down on the top step and peered at the keyhole. She could see light, so Faith had obviously taken the key with her. Tara pushed the knife attachment into the gap and tried to find a space to lever it aside. But it was too stiff. The small knife just jabbed at the wood around the lock, uselessly.

She kept trying for several minutes until tears of frustration were running down her face. It was hopeless. They were trapped in here.

Melodie still lay on her front, apparently in some kind of shock. Tara remembered she had only just heard Will was dead. In normal life she would have felt compassion for the other girl, but normal life seemed like something that was too far in the past to remember.

'Is there any other way out of here at all?' she said harshly.

Melodie shook her head, barely perceptibly. She muttered something too quiet for Tara to hear.

'What?'

'I hate her,' said Melodie in a trembling voice. 'I hate her!' She burst into more noisy tears.

Tara tried to tune her out. She was thinking about people on telly who picked locks. Was it really possible? It was worth another try. She'd done it with the locker, and this building was pretty old.

She inserted the knife directly into the keyhole and pressed it sideways as far as she could get it to go. The handle dug painfully into her hand but she pressed harder and wiggled it gently. Nothing happened. This wasn't working. But she had to keep trying . . .

Please, please open . . .

CLICK.

CHAPTER 17

BREATHE

Tara sucked in her breath as the door gently swung wide. She was looking at the garden. It was twilight and a low mist was hanging over the weedy mass of the lawn. The cool fresh air on her face was delicious. The greenery of the garden, tangled and overgrown as it was, was more beautiful than anything Tara had ever seen.

It was *freedom*.

Almost.

Melodie had turned her head to the side and was watching now through slitted eyes in a puffy, tear-streaked face.

'C'mon,' said Tara quietly. 'We have to get out of here now.'

Melodie scrambled to her feet fast, surprising Tara. She raced up the stairs.

Tara went first, stepping out onto the damp grass. The weeping willow trailed over the raised hump of the shelter and she could understand now why it hadn't been visible before. Drips of water from the long green fronds plopped onto her head but she didn't mind because she was *outside*.

'Can we get to the road through the garden?' she whispered.

Melodie shook her head hard.

Tara walked to the side of the shelter towards the riverbank. A long fence ran across the length of the garden. It was curled with barbed wire and tangled with viciously thorned blackberry bushes between the garden and the water. She would be cut to pieces if she tried to climb over it.

She took a deep, quivery breath as she looked around. The French windows were open a little into the kitchen, and no lights were on inside.

They would have to go through the house.

Tara and Melodie exchanged looks. Tara tipped her head at the doors and Melodie nodded in silent understanding.

Soundlessly, the two girls moved quickly down the garden. It was torture not to run at full pelt but Tara forced herself to be careful, watching out for anything in the long grass that could trip her up or make a noise.

When they reached the doors, Tara peered into the gloomy kitchen. Some kind of mournful piano music was playing quietly in another room. Slipping inside the kitchen, her heartbeat ratcheted up, so loud she was sure it echoed in the otherwise silent space. The fridge suddenly hummed and shuddered, sending shock hurtling up Tara's spine.

'Come on,' she mouthed at Melodie and the other girl looked back at her with swollen eyes. Tara could hear her frightened breaths, in and out, like old-fashioned bellows.

Tara took a step forwards.

Her head throbbed with a pounding hum and her mouth was dry and woolly. She longed to be able to walk to the tap and pour herself a glass of cold water but instead forced herself to take careful, slow steps forward. Melodie followed closely behind.

They passed an open door to the left and Tara glanced in, flinching. Faith was lying on a red velvet sofa. A white throw shot with gold was hanging off and pooling on the floor. Her arm hung down to the ground, her small fingers curled elegantly inwards. Faith was so still, Tara wondered hopefully if she was dead. Then a loud snore emanated from the doll-like figure and she muttered something unintelligible. Tara and Melodie froze. But Faith became still once again.

Tara breathed out slowly and her limbs weakened with relief. *Thank God* . . .

And then the tinny sound of dance music exploded

217

through the still air, shockingly loud. Faith's mobile phone was on a glass coffee table. It was moving slightly as though dancing to the music.

Faith sat straight up and stared directly at Tara with a confused expression.

Melodie pushed past her, strong suddenly, as she got to the front door. She wrenched it open and was out but then Faith seemed to come from nowhere, slamming the door shut before Tara could get out too. The phone was still ringing and then it stopped abruptly. The landline began to ring. Tara expected to hear Melodie battering on the door on the other side but the only sound was her own breathing and the phone, ringing over and over again.

Melodie had gone. She had left Tara here alone.

'You silly little bitch,' said Faith, her voice surprisingly clear. If she had been drunk before, she was sober now. 'You made it all go wrong, coming here,' she continued in a hiss. 'Ross only panicked because of you.' Her eyes filled with tears.

Tara had never hit anyone properly in her life but now she swung her fist in an instinctive punch. Faith was too quick though and ducked. Tara hit the door instead and pain blasted through her knuckles.

'What do you want from me?' she sobbed. 'Let me go! It's all over now. Don't you know that they're coming to get you?'

'Shut up!' screamed Faith. 'Shut up, shut up!' Her mouth was twisted with rage and her lips stained with red wine.

And then Faith moved so fast that Tara didn't even have time to blink. She was falling backwards onto the wooden floor of the hall and something was over her face, taking her breath away. Something white and soft. A pillow. Faith was trying to smother her with a pillow.

Tara shoved at the weight on top of her, fighting with every last bit of her strength but she was tired and sore and dizzy and anyway, Faith was gripping like a limpet, stronger than she should be for her size. Tara's head thrashed from side to side, trying to clear a space for air, desperately trying to pummel the woman on top of her. But Faith was sitting astride her chest and all Tara could do was flap and try to make contact with the woman's back. It wasn't making any difference. She couldn't get free. Faith was small but possessed with the strength of a person who no longer had anything to lose. She'd killed two people already. What difference would another make?

This realisation squeezed the last remaining air from Tara's lungs. Her chest cramped and ached and lights began to explode inside her mind. She thought about Leo and the lido. She remembered the cool blue world underwater and wished she'd never, ever wasted air.

She was going to die here. She'd never see her family again.

Mum, Dad, Beck . . . Sammie . . .

Play dead.

She didn't know where the words came from. But a split second later she forced herself to go limp, her feet flopping to the sides.

It was just enough to make Faith slacken her grip a little. Pulling the last trickle of strength from somewhere deep inside, Tara twisted sideways, gulping air into her screaming lungs and slamming Faith against the wall of the hallway.

The front door opened with a crash then and people flooded the hallway. Everyone was shouting and bodies seemed to fill the space. Somewhere in the background a dog was barking insistently. Strong arms were lifting her up and there was a crackle of static and noise that hurt her head.

Someone shouted 'Tara!' and someone else yelled, 'Get away from her, son! She might be injured!'

Tara couldn't get her eyes to focus properly. Everything was blurred and distorted.

'Are you all right? Tara, are you all right? *Oh God...*'

Leo?

Her vision began to return. Leo was close, looking into her face. He was crying. He touched her cheeks and hair, delicately, checking her.

Tara's chest hurt so much. Had to breathe. In and out.

'It's okay! You're okay! You're okay!' Leo was saying the words over and over again.

Tara closed her eyes.

And let herself breathe.

EPILOGUE

The first day passed in a haze of sleep and
painkillers.

Tara was kept in hospital for five days in total.
She had concussion, bruised ribs, severe bruising to her
knuckles and was mildly dehydrated. Mum, Dad and
Beck stayed with her on rotation and Mum even slept on
a camp bed next to her for the first two nights.

Ross survived the stab wound, which turned out to
be 'relatively superficial' according to a policeman
whose name Tara kept forgetting. As soon as she'd been
able to sit up and speak, he and a colleague had made
her go over what had happened in so much detail, she'd
have screamed if she only had the energy. Faith was in
custody, charged with murder and GBH. Tara told the

police as much as she could, but she left out the pictures in her mind. They didn't need to know that detail. Anyway, the precise order of events was still a muddle to Tara. She knew that distraught Melodie had run to the next-door neighbour who'd called the police. But Leo was there too. He'd gone to see Faith and found Sammie. He must have guessed that Tara was inside the house.

She still didn't know exactly what had happened because Leo didn't come to the hospital. She kept looking, hopefully, at the doors to the ward when visiting hours began.

But still he didn't come. A heavy sadness filled the pit of her stomach every time a person appeared that wasn't him. She tried to concentrate on her few good memories, shuffling the pack in an attempt to stop the horrible pictures that constantly sneaked into her mind.

That wine bottle coming towards her.

Waking up in the bomb shelter and seeing Faith sitting there, so cold and cruel.

And the pillow over her face as her last breaths ebbed away . . .

Mum said there would be counselling for her as soon as she left the hospital, but all she wanted really was to see Leo.

But maybe what they'd had was too fragile to survive this . . .

She did have one surprising visitor on the fourth day.

It was late afternoon. Mum was thoroughly getting on her nerves. When the pictures of Faith first came into her dreams and Tara jerked awake, crying, she was grateful for the presence at the side of the bed. But after a couple of days, the events in that house were starting to take on a hazy quality and details were blurring at the edges. And Tara was grateful for that. People kept saying she was going to need counselling and maybe she would, later. But now she was getting itchy for her own things. For home. Plus, Mum kept looking at Tara as though trying to memorise every inch of her face. Her eyes filled with tears on a frequent basis and she constantly blew her nose. It was becoming a little wearing.

So it was a relief when Beck turned up. He persuaded Mum he'd keep Tara company while Mum got some chores done at home.

He made himself comfortable in the chair next to Tara's bed, rummaged in her box of chocolates and checked messages on his phone, evidently untroubled by any need to make conversation.

Tara gave a small grin at her oblivious big brother. He carried an air of the outside world with him that made her deeply envious and grateful at the same time.

The curtain around her bed was half closed on the side nearest the door. When it was yanked suddenly, Tara expected to see yet another nurse or doctor wanting to check her head wound or her blood pressure or the other million things they did on an almost hourly basis.

But it wasn't a nurse or doctor. It was Karis, looking at her with wide eyes. She clutched a bunch of flowers and a bag of grapes. She smiled weakly at Tara and then spotted Beck and her cheeks instantly coloured. Tara was impressed, despite herself, that Karis hadn't immediately started batting her eyelashes. If anything, she looked uncomfortable and her eyes slid away back to Tara's face. She smiled again.

'Hope you don't mind that I've come to see you,' she said quietly.

Beck looked up and did that split-second appraising thing that boys didn't think girls could even see. He smiled.

'Who's this then?' he said and Karis swallowed, glanced at him and then back at Tara.

'This is Karis, from school,' said Tara, sitting up. 'Beck . . . ?'

Beck got up and beamed the full wattage of his smile at Karis. He may even have winked. 'No problem,' he said, sauntering off.

Karis looked a bit pained. 'I don't want you to think I came here because of him,' she said.

Tara surprised herself with a small laugh. It felt like the first laugh in a long time.

'It's okay, I wasn't thinking that,' she said.

Karis seemed to visibly relax. She placed the flowers and grapes on the table at the bottom of Tara's bed and then perched awkwardly on the chair, as though she might flee at any second.

'Have a chocolate,' said Tara, holding the box Beck had been plundering towards Karis, who shook her head but smiled gratefully. 'Although I'm not sure my greedy brother has left many.'

'How . . . how are you feeling?' she said tentatively.

'I'm all right,' said Tara. 'Bit bored now.'

A long pause stretched out.

'I suppose they're having a field day at school,' said Tara.

Karis met her eyes and then looked down at her lap. 'It's mainly Mel they're talking about, to be honest.'

'Oh?' Tara's belly gave a little quiver as she imagined running the gamut of faces hungry for gossip back at school. 'But they know I was there?'

'Yeah, course,' said Karis, 'but everyone knows you got involved because you're with Leo. And that you were trying to help.'

Tara sank back into her pillows, tired suddenly. She seemed to get so exhausted lately. It was hard to imagine how she would be able to go to school and do normal things again.

'Why did you come then, Karis?' she said. Almost being murdered had a very liberating effect, she was finding. She didn't really care what anyone thought about her at the moment, although she was aware that might not last. 'Was it to get the juicy details?'

'No!' Karis's cheeks flushed. 'It really isn't anything like that! It's just . . .' She swallowed. 'I could have been nicer, that's all. When you started. It must have been hard, you know, starting in Year Ten. When everyone knows each other.'

Tara regarded the other girl. 'Yeah,' she said quietly. 'It was.' There was another pause. 'So what has Jada been saying about me?'

Karis rolled her eyes. 'She keeps trying to come out with some stupid story about you being psychic or something but no one is listening to her. What happened to Mel . . . and you . . . well, it's kind of bigger news than anything she has to say, you know?'

Tara felt a slow grin wrap itself around her mouth. 'Right.'

'Anyway,' said Karis getting to her feet. 'I can't really stay because my dad's coming to get me. But I wanted to say, you know, sorry . . . and that maybe when you're back on your feet . . . maybe you could come round to mine one day. You know . . . only if you wanted to.'

Tara smiled up at her. 'Thanks, I'd like that,' she said shyly.

'Okay, then,' Karis said, returning her grin.

'Going so soon?' Beck came back around the side of the curtain, holding three cans of Coke.

Tara rolled her eyes at Karis and the other girl burst out laughing.

'Something I said?' Beck settled himself back into the newly vacated chair and reached for the chocolates.

A few days later, Tara was home.

Mum – and Dad – were driving her nuts with their

requests about how she was feeling, so she decided to take a walk down to the river. She wasn't strong enough to take Sammie yet and the dog gazed at her balefully as she left the house without him.

Autumn had arrived in full force now and the river was covered with gold and red leaves like scales. The sky was iron grey and it was hard to imagine that she'd swum outdoors only a couple of weeks before. The year was turning. Everything was changing.

She was sitting on the bench looking at the water when footsteps behind made her turn. Her heart flipped over.

'Oh,' she said. 'Hi.'

Leo stood a few metres away, hands in his pockets and a shy half-smile on his face.

'No mutt today?' he said quietly. 'No Sammie?'

'What, suddenly you like my dog?' said Tara weakly.

Leo smiled a little and took another few steps closer.

'I wouldn't go that far,' he said, 'but we had to spend time together and we, you know, worked through a few issues. I had a word about the bad breath and the whole crotch-sniffing thing.'

'Oh yeah?' Tara felt a smile tug at her lips.

'Yeah,' said Leo. They looked at each other for a moment and then the connection between their eyes was broken.

'Can I sit there?' said Leo uncertainly.

Tara looked down. 'Yeah, if you want.'

She felt awkward, suddenly hyper-conscious of how

pale and washed out she still looked. And she didn't know how to be with him. He hadn't come to see her in hospital, had he?

'How are you feeling?' he said quietly.

Tara felt a surge of resentment, powerful and hot, towards him. It came out of nowhere.

'I'm all right,' she said tersely. 'They did a good job. You know. In hospital.' She looked into his eyes and knew her message was getting across just fine.

He flushed, attractively. Why did it always look so cute when he did it? It didn't seem very fair, when blushing turned Tara's whole head scarlet. But she wasn't blushing now. She felt too angry.

'I did try to come and see you,' he said quietly.

'Oh,' said Tara. 'What? I mean, when? And why didn't I see you?'

Leo put his hands in his pockets and looked towards the river. He coughed and Tara got the sensation that he was deeply uncomfortable.

'I bumped into your brother,' he said, his voice still low and quiet. 'Beck, is it?'

Tara nodded, watching him. 'And . . . did he say something to you?'

Leo laughed. 'Kind of, yeah.' He took an audible breath in. 'Said my family was poison and that if I caused you a day's more upset, he'd . . . not be happy. Spelt out what he'd do. Very clearly . . .' He shrugged.

'Idiot,' muttered Tara under her breath. She'd be having a word with her big brother later, the cheeky sod.

'I'm not planning to hurt you,' Leo continued, 'but then I started thinking he was right. It's true, isn't it? It was my family that did this to you, after all.' He lifted his hand and, with a feather-light finger, brushed the side of her forehead where the bruise was now fading to a sickly yellow. 'So maybe I should stay away. Maybe we *are* poison.'

They looked into each other's eyes. Tara's insides tumbled and twisted as though she was being shaken up. She swallowed.

'It wasn't your fault,' she whispered. 'I don't blame *you*.'

Tara watched the hope blossom in Leo's eyes. They held each other's gaze and then both broke away and stared at the river.

'How's, um, your sister?' said Tara after a moment, needing to fill the silence.

'She's all right,' said Leo gruffly. 'She's gone to Brighton for real now. Seems she might have been in trouble for agreeing to the kidnap thing, but they're not pressing charges because of her age.'

'Oh, right,' said Tara.

A bitter image of Melodie yelling, 'Do it to her!' scrolled across her mind. She'd *helped* that girl. Or had she made things worse? It was hard to know now.

Leo cleared his throat, bringing Tara back into the moment. She kept doing this since everything happened. Zoning out. Her cheeks flooded with heat and she bit her lip.

'Anyway . . .' he began.

Tara glanced at him. His long legs were stretched out in front of him, his hands in his pockets. It may have looked cocky, but the way he swallowed and coughed again suggested he wasn't feeling cocky after all.

'What I should have said to Beck . . . and what I'm saying to you now . . . is that I, you know, I have another family,' he said. 'Mel's my sister and always will be. And she's messed up, badly. But what I'm trying to say is, me and my dad, we're not connected to . . . to Faith.'

Tara didn't know what to say. Silence hung heavily between them.

'I'm not making any sense,' he continued, 'but I came to say I'm sorry you got caught up in it. And that I'm not like them. I'll understand if you want to tell me to get lost. You probably don't want to see me again anyway. And there's the leisure centre if you ever go swimming again.'

Leo sighed. 'I just needed to get that off my chest in case there was any chance, um . . .' His voice trailed away. He looked directly into her eyes now. Tara saw sadness and longing there and felt an almost magnetic pulling sensation in her body towards him.

'It's all right,' she said shyly. 'I don't blame you for any of it.'

Leo turned to her, his face radiating hope. She could kiss him now if she wanted to. She knew that with absolute certainty. But as much as she wanted to throw her arms around his neck she knew they weren't finished with this conversation yet. There was stuff she needed to say. Tara felt she'd spent too long trying to hide away. Trying to pretend she was someone else.

'This . . . thing of mine?' she said, forcing strength into her words. 'You know . . . the thing I told you about. How I knew Melodie was in trouble . . .'

Leo's eyebrows knitted in confusion. 'What about it?'

'Well . . .' Tara swallowed. 'Doesn't that . . . put you off? Doesn't it bother you?'

'Bother me?' he parroted.

'Yes!' she said, her voice rising with frustration. 'I mean, it's not exactly normal is it?'

Leo laughed. A genuine, easy laugh. 'Normal's overrated,' he said. 'And anyway . . . maybe I'm not the best judge, when you think about it.'

Tara felt a slow grin spread across her lips. Leo was grinning back at her, his eyes shining.

'So . . .' he said in not much more than a whisper. 'What do you think? About . . . everything?' He spread his hands.

Tara took a deep breath. 'Well . . . I like the *lido*,' she said, scrunching her face and pretending to think it through. 'I like the challenge of taking my life in my hands when I go swimming, what with all the hazardous materials. And anyway, I'm still holding out for the sight of Dobby in his swimming trunks.'

Leo laughed. They met eyes again. Time felt suspended between them.

'Oh for God's sake, come here will you!' said Tara at last. She threw her arms around his neck, pulling him in for a kiss. Leo's arms snaked around her back and drew her closer.

A cool breeze ruffled the surface of the river.

People walked past, their feet crackling the leaves that covered the path. Glancing at the entwined teenagers on the bench, they smiled at each other.

But Tara didn't notice.

She was lost.

Acknowledgements

My editor Anne Clark was invaluable in helping shape *Dark Ride* and *Cracks* and the same holds true for this book. Thank you, Anne, for your brilliant editorial eye and friendship.

A big thank you to my sister Helenanne Hansen for being an early reader of *Hold Your Breath* and giving me a boost of confidence that the story was going in the right direction.

Andrew Roach sent me some wonderful photos of the river near his house, which was the inspiration for the one that flows through Tara's town. Thanks, Andy!

Thanks also to Benjamin at the Arundel Lido and Maureen Saunders at the Beccles Lido for their help with a couple of technical questions about outdoor swimming pools.

As ever, Luisa Plaja, Emily Gale and Alexandra Fouracres have been there with their unending support (and laughs).

I'm very honoured to be part of a writing group that includes Emma Darwin, Margot Watts, Linda Buckley-Archer, Susannah Cherry and Essie Fox. Thank you, Daily Breaders, for letting me be part of your talented gang.

I've already dedicated the book to my wonderful group of students at East Barnet School (hey, remember to invite me to your own book launches one day) but I would also like to thank staff and students there generally. Working as your Writer in Residence this year has been a real pleasure.

I also want to say a big thank you to my father, George Green for his generosity and for always believing in me.

Thanks also to my agent Catherine Pellegrino for her continuing support.

Pete, Joe and Harry always come at the end of the list of acknowledgements but nowhere has the phrase 'last but not least' been most apt. Love you, guys. You make me feel lucky every day.